GUARDIAN GHOST

GUARDIAN GHOST

Christine Nostlinger

Translated by Anthea Bell

Andersen Press · London

First published in 1986 by
Andersen Press Limited,
62-65 Chandos Place, London WC2

First published in English in 1986.

Originally published in German as *Rosa Riedl, Schutzgespenst* by Jugend und Volk Verlagsgesellschaft m.b.H., Vienna, Austria.

British Library Cataloguing in Publication Data
Nostlinger, Christine
Guardian ghost.
I. Title II. Rosa Riedl Schutzgespenst.
English
833'.914[J] PZ7

ISBN 0-86264-152-7

Printed and bound in Great Britain by
Anchor Brendon Limited, Tiptree, Essex

1

Rosa Riedel was mixed up with a great many people. Not just Tina and Stacey. One way or another, a whole block of apartment buildings got involved with this story. Take Mrs Wokurka, for instance, caretaker of Number 44, Geyergasse. She would have said the story should begin at nine o'clock one Sunday morning in 1944. That was when all the jam jars on the top shelf of her dresser began to wobble. Then one jar actually jumped off the shelf, almost hitting the ceiling. And then it went floating across the kitchen, keeping just below the ceiling, and upon reaching the fanlight above the kitchen door, which was open, it floated out into the corridor and away. You could have knocked her down with a feather, said Mrs Wokurka later. She was scared stiff. Struck by a bolt of icy lightning, that was the way she felt. It was only when the sirens began howling that she was able to move again and run down to the cellar. (1944 was wartime. Whenever American planes flew over the sirens howled, warning people to go down to their cellars and shelter from air raids.)

She had three of these strange experiences, said Mrs Wokurka. Next autumn, two farm eggs left by way of her kitchen fanlight, and a piece of bacon went in winter. Mrs Wokurka had been keeping the bacon hidden in a cupboard, because it was forbidden to have any bacon at the time. (You couldn't buy bacon except on the black market, and black market goods were particularly strictly forbidden.)

Mrs Wokurka distinctly saw the cupboard open of its own accord, and the bacon came out. Mrs Wokurka tried to catch the bacon. She minded a great deal about that bacon. She had given the farmer a winter coat and a new silk nightie for it. But the bacon was not to be caught. Mrs Wokurka even shouted, 'Stop!' but that did no good. The bacon flew out of the fanlight, just like those two eggs and her jar of apricot jam.

'Supposing times had been different,' says Mrs Wokurka now, 'well, stands to reason I'd have kicked up a fuss, wouldn't I?' But in those days, says Mrs Wokurka, you couldn't really do that. There was a lot worse happening in those days than the odd item of food sailing through the air. And anyway, people were used to keeping their mouths shut in those days.

'Didn't hardly dare say anything, did we?' she says now. 'Didn't dare say you didn't fancy the war, nor Hitler, nor yet seeing your apricot jam floating about!' Moreover, Mrs Wokurka could have been locked up if she had mentioned the matter. Either on suspicion of being crazy, or for having eggs and bacon. They could even have got her for having sugar to make the apricot jam, because the tiny sugar ration you were allowed then wasn't enough for jam-making.

However, with respect to Mrs Wokurka and her floating food, this story will get too complicated if we go right back to 1944. We would have to bring bombs and ration books into it, and frightened people sheltering in cellars, and the arrival of the Russians and the Americans in Austria, and the 'reconstruction' of the country, and you would have to read a hundred pages before the story ever got to Tina and Stacey.

We will just say, then, that many, many years ago Mrs Wokurka felt as if she had been struck by a bolt of icy lightning. (And at the same time, on three separate occasions, once in May, once in autumn and once in winter, Mrs Sedlak had a delightful, wonderful surprise. Mrs

Sedlak lived next to Mrs Wokurka. She had her three delightful, wonderful surprises when a jar of apricot jam, two eggs, and a piece of genuine farm-cured bacon came floating through her fanlight.

'A person that goes asking questions in times like these is liable to starve,' said Mrs Sedlak to herself, when it happened, and she put apricot jam on Hans's bread, and boiled the eggs for Kathi, and gave Grandfather the bacon. But she never told anyone about it. In those days, as Mrs Sedlak agrees, it was always best to keep your mouth shut.)

So I think I had better begin the story in 1978, when Mrs Wokurka was sixty-two, and Tina and Stacey were eleven. Tina's surname was Wokurka as well, because Mrs Wokurka was her grandmother. Stacey's name was Sommer, and she didn't have a grandmother.

And as this looks like being a pretty short Chapter 1, I may as well explain how I come to know so much about the story. The reason is that I am inquisitive, and I live in the block of apartment buildings next to the block where Stacey and Tina and Mrs Sedlak and Mrs Wokurka live, along with all the other people who found themselves mixed up with Rosa Riedel.

2

Tina and Stacey's was a friendship of convenience. (They were the same age, and in the same class at school, and they lived in the same block of buildings.)

When Stacey felt bored, she could look out of her kitchen window straight into Tina's kitchen window opposite. Then she yelled, 'Tina!' She dared not yell anything else. (This was because of Miss Dostal, who lived below Stacey and got cross if people shouted at each other across the back yards. 'Common,' she called it. Miss Dostal herself was very refined; she even wore gloves in summer. She talked in a refined way too, telling the greengrocer, 'Ay would laike a bunch of chaives, please!')

Because of Miss Dostal, then, Tina and Stacey had invented a secret sign language. (Hand to mouth meant: I'm bored! Thumb turned down meant: Coming out in the yard? Thumb on chest meant: Come over to my place! Knocking forehead with fist meant: Haven't done my homework yet.)

In summertime, when Stacey and Tina stood at their kitchen windows, their thumbs were generally to be observed pointing downwards, and shortly afterwards they might be seen in the yard below.

There was a wooden fence between Tina's back yard and Stacey's back yard. It had had a plank missing for years. Stacey could get through this gap into Tina's back yard. It didn't work the other way around, Tina being twice as fat as Stacey. However, that didn't matter, since Tina's yard was prettier anyway. Stacey's contained nothing but three dustbins, a carpet-beating pole, a chopping block and a spindly lilac bush.

But Tina's back yard was a real garden. There was a tiny lawn, about the size of a kitchen floor, and rose bushes, and a plaster garden gnome holding a lantern. And then there was the arbour, which had Virginia creeper growing all over it. The leaves of the creeper were so thick that no one could see inside the arbour until they fell, late in the autumn. They hung across the front of the arbour too, and you had to stoop down to get into it.

Tina and Stacey liked sitting in this arbour. They often had Mrs Sedlak's old cat in there with them, and sometimes old Franz's dog arrived as well. Old Franz lived in Stacey's building. The dog got through the gap in the fence, like Stacey.

When she saw old Franz's dog making for the arbour, Stacey would say, 'I'll have to go home now!' And she slipped out of the arbour and through the gap in the fence and back home. Stacey was scared of that dog, but she couldn't admit it, because the dog was so tiny. Tina wouldn't even have understood a person being scared of big dogs. Tina loved all dogs! Tina would pat St. Bernards who were total strangers to her in the street, and was quite happy to open garden gates with Rottweilers or boxers growling the other side of them. Tina wasn't scared of anything at all.

Stacey, unfortunately, was always scared. Not just of dogs, both large and small: she was also scared of cellars, being alone, attics and mysterious noises. Stacey was scared to be alone in her room in the dark, when a car went by in the street, because it sent a strip of light travelling over the ceiling. She was scared of the floor in her room too. It sometimes creaked and groaned, entirely of its own accord.

The evenings when Stacey's parents went out were worst of all. They used to have a babysitter for her, but babysitters cost money, and anyway they were just for babies. At the end of Class 4 at school, when Stacey came back from the summer holidays with her parents, her dad said he thought she was old enough to be left on her own in the evenings now.

'We'll give it a try, shall we?' he suggested.

'We'll only be out for a couple of hours,' Mum said.

Those two hours were dreadful to Stacey. She lay in bed, terrified of the lights from cars and the creaking floor. She needed to go to the lavatory, but she didn't dare. She was hungry, but she dared not go to the kitchen. Then the telephone rang, and Stacey jumped with fright at every ring. She couldn't have got out of bed to answer that phone for the world.

When her parents came back, after exactly two hours four minutes, they asked, 'Not too bad, was it, Stacey dear?'

'No, it was fine!' said Stacey, and she hurried off to the lavatory, and found herself something to eat, and pretended she had spent two nice, peaceful hours on her own.

After that Stacey's parents went out in the evenings twice a week. Usually on Tuesdays and Fridays. That made Tuesdays and Fridays terrible days for Stacey. She was green with envy when Tina said happily, 'I'm in luck today. My mum and dad are going round to friends, so I can watch telly till closedown!' Stacey was also green with envy when she heard of Tina fetching potatoes up from the cellar, or going down to empty the rubbish in the evening, when it was dark.

One Friday, when Stacey's parents were at a party and Tina's had gone out to the pub, Tina suggested meeting late in the evening in the arbour.

'It'll be ever so romantic, Stacey,' she said. 'We can bring a torch, and biscuits, and Coca-Cola, and we'll tell each other scary stories!'

All that Friday, Stacey firmly intended to go out to the arbour in the evening. 'I do dare, I do!' she kept telling herself in a whisper. But when her parents were actually gone, Stacey stood in the hall, behind the front door, and opened it just a crack. The curly banisters cast alarming shadows on the stairs. And somebody had forgotten to shut the attic door. The attic door, one floor up from Stacey, was open, and as a window had also been left open on the stairs, and there was a slight breeze, the attic door was swinging back and forth, squealing. And then Mr Karl coughed, down on the ground floor, but Stacey felt someone was coughing right into her ear. She slammed the door, fast, got into bed fully dressed, and pulled the covers up over her head.

Tina was very cross next day. 'You beast!' she said furiously, on the way to school. 'I waited half an hour. I whistled for you, too!'

Stacey said she was sorry, but she'd had a visitor. A nice uncle she hadn't seen for ages, so he was more important.

'Well, you might at least have told me!' said Tina crossly. 'A couple of minutes wouldn't have hurt!'

Tina went on being cross all Saturday and Sunday, and was not on normal speaking terms with Stacey again until Monday. Even then she said, once or twice, 'I'm not forgetting Friday, you know! I'd never have thought you could be so mean!'

Stacey just shrugged her shoulders and looked snooty. (She could do that quite easily. Stacey sometimes looked snooty even when she didn't want to. It was something about her face. She had a pretty face, but it wasn't a cheerful, child-like face. Pepi Schestak, who lived in Tina's building, called her the Princess on the Pea. Mr Karl said, 'Stacey has a distinguished face.' People with distinguished faces can't help it if other people think they are snooty.)

In any case, Stacey preferred being thought snooty to being thought cowardly; least of all did she want Tina to know how scared she got, because Tina laughed at scaredy-cats. Tina enjoyed frightening little Pepi too. Sometimes she lay in wait for Pepi down in the hall, behind the front door of the building, and when he came in she jumped out at him going, 'Boo!' and was pleased to see him run away howling.

'It even pays off, Stacey!' she had told her friend not long ago. 'Last time I scared Pepi, he dropped a packet of chewing gum when he ran away!'

And Tina showed Stacey the packet of gum. She was going to give Stacey a piece, too, but Stacey said she didn't want any.

3

Stacey couldn't explain why she was so scared of anything and everything, but she had recently found out why Tina feared nothing at all. If Tina had not been so round and fat, Stacey would have discovered long before. However, Tina always wore high-necked clothes to cover all her rolls of fat. Even her leotard for gym had a polo neck.

But now that it was winter, Tina and Stacey had swimming instead of gym in the afternoons, so Tina had to take her polo-neck sweater off, and then Stacey saw that she had a little gold chain around her neck, wedged between two rolls of fat. A thin little chain with a pendant. There was nothing special about that in itself. Lots of children have chains with pendants on them: a silver Charlie Brown, or a golden football, or an enamel Asterix. Stacey had even seen tiny Ferris wheels and miniature playing cards hanging from chains.

But the pendant on Tina's chain was a little gold disc, enamelled on one side, with a painted head showing a child's fat-cheeked face. The head had a neck with two tiny sky-blue wings growing out of it.

Stacey pulled the pendant out of the rolls of fat and admired it. She liked it, but she had no idea what the winged head was supposed to be.

'It's my guardian angel,' Tina had told her. 'It looks after me. But you wouldn't understand. You don't go to Religious Instruction.'

Stacey said no more. She looked snooty again—on purpose this time.

Stacey asked no questions about guardian angels at home, either. Stacey's parents didn't even believe in angels, so how could they know about a sub-division, the guardian sort?

Stacey took her questions about guardian angels to Mrs Berger, one of the neighbours. Mrs Berger was old and kind. She knew all about guardian angels. She showed Stacey three. One was on another pendant, and looked like the twin of Tina's. The other two—they were in books—were long, pale, thin guardian angels with large feathery wings. One of them was keeping watch beside a baby's cot. The other was floating along beside a toddler happily crossing a narrow bridge. There was a vast waterfall underneath the bridge.

Stacey remembered last summer holidays, when they went to Scotland. Right behind the hotel where they were staying there had been a waterfall like that, with a bridge over it, except that the bridge was broader and the waterfall smaller than in the book with guardian angels. Stacey remembered how scared she had always been, crossing that bridge over the waterfall. She couldn't do it unless Dad was holding her hand. Mum's hand wouldn't do. Stacey longed to have one of those guardian angels. She didn't mind whether it was a fat-cheeked little one, or a tall thin one. But Mrs Berger explained that it was no use just going into a shop and buying an angel pendant. 'You have to believe in it,' she said.

'But I do believe in it,' said Stacey. However, Mrs Berger explained that you can't just believe in guardian angels. If the guardian angel is really going to work, you have to believe in everything else to do with religion as well. You have to be a devout, pious person, who goes to church every Sunday, and confesses sins, and takes Communion, and in general leads a good Christian life.

'But your family don't go to church at all, do they?' said Mrs Berger. And then, seeing how sad Stacey suddenly looked, she added comfortingly, 'I don't think that matters though. You carry right on believing in guardian angels, and I'm sure they'll help you.' Stacey realized this was just meant to be a comfort. Stacey was not stupid. She could always tell when people meant what they said. So she was still sad, even though Mrs Berger gave her both the guardian angel books, and promised her the angel pendant for her next birthday.

Stacey went home and sat down in her room and read the guardian angel books, but there wasn't much about guardian angels in them. They were full of poems and little prayers, that was all. Later on, Stacey's mother saw the angel books, and laughed a lot. Amusingly slushy old stuff, she said they were. And when Stacey's father came home, Mum read some of the poems out loud, still laughing a lot, and Dad laughed even more. And finally they said it was a good thing times were different now and nobody expected small children to believe such nonsense.

'Are guardian angels nonsense, then?' Stacey asked Dad, and Dad shrugged his shoulders. 'Believing in them doesn't hurt if people want to,' he said. But Stacey's mum said she thought poorly of guardian angels, and they only did harm. 'Where would we be if children trusted to guardian angels in a busy street?' she said. 'You have to learn traffic sense for yourself or you get run over.' And Stacey's Dad added, 'Yes, and what about the children who've had accidents, then? What about the poor children who died? Were their guardian angels asleep at the time, or what?'

Stacey had to admit that Mum and Dad were right in a way. But she still wished she had a guardian angel. Sometimes, when her longing for a guardian angel was very bad, for instance on those dreadful Tuesdays and Fridays, Stacey sat down at her desk, put her head on the desk top, and whispered quietly to herself, 'I want a guardian angel!

Oh please, I do need a guardian angel! How come Tina has a guardian angel and not me?'

4

Next week, after swimming, Stacey and Tina had a quarrel. It began in the changing rooms, while they were dressing. Tina was in a bad temper. Stacey was combing her wet hair in front of the mirror. 'Would Miss Anastasia mind hurrying up a bit?' inquired Tina. 'Other people's hair is wet too, you know!' Although Stacey was being as quick as she could.

Then, when they were waiting for their tram, with the others, Tina said, 'I see Miss Anastasia's got a trodden-down heel!' Stacey couldn't bear being called by her full name, as Tina very well knew. And knowing it, Tina added, 'What was your mum up to anyway, giving you a name like that? Thought she was having the Tsar's youngest daughter, did she?'

Everybody standing near Stacey and Tina giggled. Except for Michael. He didn't giggle because his own first names were really Vladimir Stanislaus Michael, so he knew what it's like, having an unusual name. But one child out of two dozen not laughing was no comfort to Stacey. Maybe it would have been a comfort if she had known why Tina was in such a temper. In point of fact, Tina was cross with Stacey for being much prettier and slimmer than herself. She had noticed that yet again, and only too clearly, in the swimming baths. Stacey had also told Tina, 'You know, I think you eat too much. I'm sure you've put on another couple of pounds.' Stacey meant no harm. (But then neither did Tina mean any harm when she called Stacey a scaredy-cat.)

Stacey didn't know how to defend herself against Tina's nasty remarks, so she put her 'snooty' expression on, said, 'See you!' to Michael, and just walked off. She went down the street, towards home, wondering if she could get herself rechristened. Then it struck her that she had never been christened anyway, not in a church with a font and a clergyman, because her family were not churchgoers. And that reminded her of the guardian angel again. If I had a guardian angel, she thought, the angel would have made sure I got a proper name! I bet that's the kind of thing guardian angels are for! My guardian angel would never have let them call me Anastasia. My angel wouldn't have let me be landed a name that makes other children laugh!

Stacey worked out just how the guardian angel would have fixed it to get her a nicer name. She saw the whole thing, quite distinctly: the registry office, and Dad standing outside the door, holding a piece of paper on which Mum had written ANASTASIA in large capital letters. Dad looked at the piece of paper, shook his head, and muttered to himself, 'Well, if that's what my dear wife insists on calling our dear daughter, I suppose I must go along with it!' And then Dad knocked at the door and went into the registrar's office. But the guardian angel stole in after him without anyone noticing. A tall, pale, thin guardian angel, one of the sort with strong wings, carrying a long-stemmed lily. 'And what is the baby to be called?' the registrar asked Dad. Dad smiled and looked at his piece of paper. But the guardian angel came right up to Dad, and passed the stem of the lily very, very gently over the piece of paper, wiping out STASIA and just leaving ANA. Dad was quite bewildered. 'Er . . . Ana . . . ' he stammered, and the registrar gave him a friendly nod. Dad tried again, and he nearly managed to say it, but the guardian angel raised one wing, just a little, and flapped the wing close to Dad's mouth, wiping the 'stasia' part off his lips. And the registrar nodded again, and said, 'Congratulations, my dear sir! Anna—a beautiful name!' Thereupon the registrar wrote 'Anna' on the birth certificate, and once something's been entered on a birth certificate it's there for ever!

Just as Stacey had reached this point in the guardian angel story, something struck her left calf. It was Tina's swimming bag. 'All insulted, are we?' said Tina. 'Can't you take a joke?'

Stacey did not reply. For one thing she was indeed feeling insulted, and for another she wanted to go on working out the guardian angel story. 'You aren't half boring!' said Tina. 'Always acting insulted!' And she swung her swimming bag against Stacey's legs again. It hardly hurt at all, but it infuriated Stacey, and she shouted, 'You just leave me alone, you silly cow!'

'Who's a silly cow then?' Tina shouted back. 'You're a pig, you're a goose! Silly cow yourself!' And this time she hit Stacey's legs so hard with her bag that it really did hurt. She put her tongue out too, and punched Stacey in the ribs with the hand which was not holding the swimming bag.

Stacey wondered if she could risk getting into a fight. On the one hand, Tina was twice as fat and at least twice as strong as Stacey, but on the other hand they were only ten paces or so from the front door of Stacey's building.

Stacey decided that she could risk the fight. First she took two big steps, shouting, 'You shut up, you great fat balloon!' Then she took two more steps, getting punched in the ribs each time. Then yet another two steps, yelling, 'Go away, and I don't ever want to see you again!' Then one more step, and now it was only three more steps to the front door, so she raised her hand and slapped Tina's face.

Tina was so surprised that she dropped her swimming bag, and Stacey dashed indoors. She ran upstairs and rang the front doorbell of the apartment. Unfortunately, she had no key with her. There was no sign of life inside the apartment. (At this very moment, Stacey's mother was in the tobacconist's telling the woman behind the counter,

'Well, I must run now, or Stacey will be home from swimming, and she can't get in!') Stacey rang and rang. Then she began ringing the bell of the apartment next door, Mrs Berger's, but there was no sign of life there either. The only sign of life was down in the hall of the building: Tina, puffing and panting crossly and making for the stairs. Stacey heard her coming up. 'I'll tell her mum of her!' Tina was saying. 'I'll tell her mum of her!'

Stacey wondered whether to run and hide in the attic, but she was as scared of the attic as she was of Tina. So she stood there, trembling a little, teeth digging into her lower lip, holding her swimming bag tightly in both hands.

When Tina reached the last floor and saw Stacey, she instantly took in the whole situation. 'Ha, ha!' said Tina, grinning. 'What, no Mummy to look after little Miss Anastasia? Russian princesses, is it?' she added. 'Just you wait!'

She put her swimming bag down on the floor and marched towards Stacey like a boxer making for his opponent. She looked as fierce and confident as a boxer too.

No point in fighting back, thought Stacey. And begging for mercy is humiliating.

Stacey closed her eyes. Any moment now she'll slap my face, thought Stacey. Any moment now she'll punch me in the stomach! Or maybe she's about to kick my shins.

But nothing at all happened. Tina did not hit her. Tina said nothing. Everything was perfectly quiet. Stacey opened her eyes again. There was Tina, right in front of her, one arm raised, motionless. She looked like some kind of monument, except that monuments can't cry.

'What's the matter, Tina?' asked Stacey in alarm. 'Aren't you feeling well? Is there something wrong?'

Tina began to sob. 'Dunno! I was going to hit you and I

lifted my arm, and now I can't move any more!'

'Don't be silly,' said Stacey.

'It's true,' wailed Tina. 'I feel as if something was holding me down. I feel it, I tell you!' Tina was bellowing her head off now. Her chin was wobbling and her teeth were chattering.

'Maybe it's cramp in your arm?' suggested Stacey. (Mrs Berger sometimes got cramp in her left leg. It was to do with her circulation, the doctor said. When Mrs Berger had cramp in her leg she couldn't move the leg either.) 'Cramp's nothing to worry about. It'll soon pass off!'

Tina collapsed on the bottom step of the flight up to the attic. She looked very funny. Sobbing, all crumpled up, but with her right arm pointing vertically upwards. Stacey tried pushing the arm down again. It was impossible. She sat down beside Tina. She had forgotten they were in the middle of a serious quarrel. She patted Tina a bit, repeating, 'It'll soon pass off, Tina!'

And then—neither of them could have said just how long the whole thing actually lasted—then Tina's arm fell back, all limp.

Tina tested her fingers to see if she could move them all properly again. She could. Her wrist and her elbow were in working order too. But there were five red spots on the white skin of her wrist: four pressure marks close together, and the fifth a little farther up, on the back of her hand.

'Does cramp do that to you?' whispered Tina. Stacey shook her head. She was sure that cramp didn't give you those red marks. You didn't get marks like that unless somebody held you tight. Pepi Schestak had once had five similiar red pressure marks on his hand, when Mrs Schestak dragged him out of the yard because he wouldn't go with her of his own accord.

Tina stared at those five red pressure marks and started

sobbing again. Just at that moment the attic door squealed, and then slammed shut with a loud bang.

Tina jumped up. 'I'm not staying here! There's something funny going on!' she cried, running downstairs.

Stacey stayed where she was, smiling to herself. She was feeling really very odd inside. She had an explanation for the five red pressure marks on Tina's hand. A lovely, nice, delightful explanation! She was sure she had just been given a guardian angel after all. In spite of not going to church. The guardian angel had held Tina's arm. The guardian angel had saved Stacey from being slapped by Tina. And once Tina had calmed down again, the guardian angel had let Tina's arm go and disappeared into the attic.

5

Tina and Stacey did not mention the episode of the raised arm and the five red pressure marks either to each other or anyone else. Stacey said nothing because she thought guardian angels wouldn't care for publicity, preferring to work undercover. Tina would have liked to talk about it. To Stacey, or Granny Wokurka, or even Pepi Schestak. But somehow she never got any farther than, 'Granny, something happened to me—' or, 'Stacey, I still don't see how—' Whenever she was about to mention it she felt as if she had suddenly been struck by a bolt of icy lightning. And as this was not a pleasant sensation, she gave up and made out she had forgotten what she was going to say. Only then did the icy feeling go away.

Stacey, however, became a little less timid daily. By Friday she had chalked up three notable acts of courage. She had walked straight past old Franz's dog without flinching. She had taken a plate of apple strudel over to Mrs Berger's even though it was getting dark out in the passage, and the banisters were casting scary shadows. On Tuesday evening, when her parents were out, she had stayed in the living room looking at all the family photograph albums.

She had not, of course, patted any St. Bernards yet. Nor had she been down to the cellar for two jars of bottled pears. I don't expect my guardian angel likes St. Bernards or cellars any more than I do, thought Stacey. (After all, guardian angels could well differ from each other. Not all guardian angels need necessarily be as brave and fearless as Tina's. Or possibly some guardian angels were just brighter than others. After all, it was freezing down in the cellar: you could easily catch cold there. And St. Bernards often have fleas, and fleas can easily jump on to people's legs, human or angelic legs, and anyone who says they can't is just a dog lover, that's all. So Stacey's guardian angel might have perfectly good, logical reasons for disliking large dogs and cold cellars!)

Then Friday evening came. Stacey's parents were invited out to supper at the Zieselhuts'. (Mum liked the Zieselhuts, Dad couldn't stand them.) The Zieselhuts liked their guests to be on time. So that morning Mum asked Dad to be sure he was home on time in the evening, and then they could set off to the Zieselhuts' punctually. Dad promised he would. (Stacey's dad was always promising things.) But Dad came home later than he'd said after all. (Stacey's dad was always coming home later than he'd said.)

When Dad arrived, Mum was standing in the hall, looking rather impatient. She already had her best coat and her going-out hat on. She was holding a bunch of flowers for Mrs Zieselhut. 'Oh, Albert, this really is the end!' she said. (Stacey's Dad's name was Albert, but Mum usually called him Bertie. She didn't say 'Albert' unless she was cross with him.)

Dad said he was sorry. He went on about the time it had taken him to find a parking place, and a discussion that lasted forever with a 'doddering old permanent secretary'. (Stacey's dad was a civil servant in a government ministry.)

Mum was still cross. 'Oh yes, we know you always have some excuse or other, Albert,' she said. She went on about his chronic unpunctuality, how he'd almost been late for his own wedding, ditto for Aunt Emma's funeral. She said he was hopelessly unreliable, and poor Mrs Zieselhut's roast would now be shrivelling up in the oven, and her rice drying out in the pan, and the other supper guests must be dying of starvation.

'Calm down,' said Dad. He added that he was ready to leave straight away, it wasn't that late yet, all he needed was half a minute to change his socks because he had a large hole in his right sock, his big toe was sticking through it and the edges of the hole hurt him.

Dad opened the sock drawer in the hall cupboard, and Mum said, 'Well, hurry up, then, Albert. This is getting ridiculous!'

Dad searched about among the socks. 'For goodness' sake,' said Mum, 'do decide which pair you want to wear, Albert!' She was tapping the floor impatiently with the toe of one shoe.

Stacey's dad was nice. Clever, and funny, with lots of other good qualities as well. But he was not even-tempered. He hated to be shouted at, and he was quite incapable of thinking: My poor dear wife has been waiting for me all this time, so no wonder she's rather cross now!

Stacey's dad was not thinking like that at all. He was thinking: That woman makes me sick! Here am I working away all day, having to argue with that senile old permanent secretary, obliged to search for parking places and wreck my nervous system just to get home anywhere near on time, and there she stands bawling me out!

While Dad thought this he was searching the drawer for two matching socks. There were at least three dozen socks in the drawer, but no one sock much resembled any other sock. And when he finally did find two which were both red, and had the same pattern, it turned out that one was considerably longer than the other. And then, when he found two white socks of the same length, one had a cable pattern and the other had a check pattern, and Dad yelled, 'That's right, carry on shouting! Go on about my unpunctuality, by all means! I suppose it's too much to expect you to see that your husband has a decent pair of socks in this drawer! Too great a strain, that'd be!' Dad was working himself up into a real rage now. 'You're at home all day,' he yelled. 'I wish I knew what you actually do with your time!'

'Oh, I sit around reading romances and eating your socks,' Mum shouted back angrily. 'I eat socks all day long, that's all I do!' Then she went to the sock drawer, being convinced that it was full of impeccable pairs of socks, but Dad just couldn't find them.

She was just reaching into the sock drawer as Dad shut it, shouting, 'Right, that's just fine, I'll wear the sock with the hole in it, and perhaps Mrs Zieselhut'll darn it for me—' But Dad got no furthur, because Mum was yelling her head off. She had caught four fingers of her right hand in the drawer as he closed it.

In the normal way Dad would now have said, 'Sorry, darling,' and Mum would have said, 'These things happen, Bertie.' But as they were both in such a temper they began quarrelling as to whether Mum was a silly cow who always had to put her fingers where they had no business, or whether Dad was a blind idiot with no consideration for the physical welfare of others.

'It's getting later and later, you know,' said Stacey. 'If you don't leave soon, Mrs Zieselhut's roast really will shrivel up.'

'The way things are right now,' said Dad, 'I couldn't care less about the Zieselhuts,' and he explained that he had only been going there to please Mum anyway, but he was not setting out to please a woman who couldn't keep his socks straight, not any more! 'I'm going to the cinema,' said Dad. 'To see a Western. With any luck it'll calm me down!' And he marched out, slamming the door behind him.

'Halfwit!' Mum shouted after him. She phoned for a taxi. 'I'll tell the Zieselhuts Dad is sick,' she told Stacey. 'I had to see to my sick husband first, that's why I'm so late!'

'What's the matter with him, then?' asked Stacey.

'I'll think of that in the taxi!' Mum kissed Stacey's cheek, and told her, 'If the Zieselhuts ring and ask why we aren't there yet, just tell them I'm on my way and Dad's not well!'

'And suppose they ask me what's wrong with him?'

'Say you're afraid you don't know!'

'But that'll make me look silly,' said Stacey.

'Then let the phone ring. You don't mind a ringing phone, do you?'

Stacey shook her head. Mum gave her another kiss on the tip of her nose, straightened her hat in front of the mirror and left the apartment. Stacey closed the front door after her and took the key out of the lock, so that it could be opened from the outside. She hung the key up on the keyboard and walked around the apartment, turning all the lights on, every last one of them! The chandeliers and the standard lamps, the bedside lamps and the lights on the walls. The fluorescent tube above the gas stove, and the globe light in the boxroom. (She and the guardian angel preferred it that way.)

Then Stacey got her knitting out of her satchel. Stacey was making a bright green ribbed sleeveless sweater in Handicrafts. The rest of the class had nearly finished their sleeveless sweaters. Stacey had knitted only seven centimetres of the back.

She turned the television on and sat down in Mum's leather TV chair with her knitting. There were ads on the telly. Stacey knitted three rows plain and three rows purl. She was very pleased with herself. She didn't feel scared at all. Going to school tomorrow, she thought, she'd tell Tina, 'I had a lovely evening yesterday! Mum and Dad were out, and I watched telly till closedown!'

Since you need something to eat and drink to feel really cosy, Stacey got up and went to the kitchen for some biscuits and Coca-Cola. There was Coke in the fridge, but it was difficult to find any really nice biscuits. Finally, right at the back of the dresser, behind the chicken brick and the potato masher and the spare candles, she found a tin of almond cookies.

Stacey put the bottle of Coke on a round tray and arranged the almond cookies around it in a circle.

When she came back into the living room with the tray, the television had stopped showing ads, and a film had begun. The credits were already over. Stacey looked for the newspaper so that she could find out what film it was from the TV programmes. (She knew from experience that there were certain films she didn't like because they gave her nightmares.) But she couldn't find the paper. She sat down in Mum's TV chair again, put an almond cookie in her mouth, took a mouthful of Coke and waited for the Coke to soften the hard biscuit, thinking: Well, if the film on the telly's a scary horror film, I can always turn it off!

There were a man and a woman on the television screen, quarrelling. It was a very angry quarrel indeed. They were not saying anything worse to each other than Stacey's Mum and Dad had said, but they were looking at each other furiously, full of hatred and dislike. Then the man slapped the woman's face, twice, and the woman began to cry and ran away.

Stacey knitted a plain row, wondering if her mum and dad could ever have such an awful quarrel, and hit each other. She decided it was quite impossible. As she thought this question over she looked down at her seventy-six green stitches. When she had finished thinking, and knitted all the bright green stitches, she looked back at the television screen.

The woman whose face had been slapped was now walking down a street. It was dark, and there was nobody else on the street, not even any cars. The woman went down it all alone, high heels tapping. She passed the front door of a building. She didn't look into the doorway, but Stacey did, and she saw a man standing there. He had pulled his hat down over his forehead and turned up the collar of his coat, and all you could see of the man himself was a staring, round eye.

Stacey dropped her knitting with fright. I must turn it off, she thought. But she was too scared to move. She had to sit there watching the man with the staring eye come out and limp along behind the woman. The woman didn't notice, though the limping, goggle-eyed man was quite close to her now.

Stacey's heart began to thud. She heard it thudding in her ears, she felt it pulsing in her throat and behind her eyes. She couldn't breathe properly any more. The downy hairs on her arms and legs rose and stood at right angles to her skin. The hair on her head stood on end too, and her scalp was crawling.

Now the goggle-eyed man reached the woman. He raised one arm. There was a sharp little knife in the hand on the end of that arm, and the music became very shrill. Then there was no music at all. The goggle-eyed man raised his arm a little higher, and the knife plunged down.

Stacey screamed. It wasn't a loud scream. It sounded like a guinea pig squeaking. If your hair is standing on end, your heart is thudding, and you are paralyzed by fright, you can't scream too well.

The woman's face was filling the screen. A face with eyes and mouth wide open.

Look away, Stacey told herself. With the very last of her strength, she turned her head aside, and saw that the door into the bedroom, which she was sure had been closed a few minutes ago, was open. And there were footprints by the door. You could see them quite clearly in the soft pile of the carpet. As if a very heavy person with size seven shoes had just been standing there. First there were only two footprints, then there were four, then six, then there was a positive trail of footprints running from the bedroom door to the television set, and then the on-off button clicked, and the dead woman's dreadful face was gone. A deep, very kind, very gentle voice asked Stacey, 'There now, ducky, what d'you want to go watching that rubbish for? You know it only scares you silly!'

Stacey's hair, the long hair on her head and the downy hair on her arms and legs, went soft and lay back down on her skin. Her heart stopped thudding and she could move again. 'Are you my guardian angel?' she asked.

There was silence for a moment, and then the voice said, 'Why, I'm Rosa Riedel, I am!' Stacey heard the sofa creak. It was an old sofa, and it always creaked when people sat down on it. Stacey looked at the sofa and the rather deep, broad dent which had appeared in the brown velvet. She felt glad and happy. That dent in the sofa, she thought, is made by my guardian angel Rosa Riedel's bottom!

'Are you a fat guardian angel with wings on your neck and nothing underneath, Rosa Riedel?' asked Stacey. (After all, the dent in the sofa could have been made by a huge head with a fat-cheeked face.) 'Or are you a tall, pale guardian angel with a lily?'

The sofa creaked a bit, the dent in the brown velvet moved slightly towards the arm of the sofa.

'And how come you're called Rosa Riedel? Mrs Berger told me angels only have first names, but not ordinary ones. They're called Gabriel, or Ezekiel, and they're not male or female but neuter.'

The sofa creaked, the dent moved towards the front of the seat, and Rosa Riedel said, 'Why, I'm no angel, I'm only

Rosa Riedel. I'm . . . well look, I don't want to scare you, do I? I know you frighten easy.'

The sofa creaked and the dent in the brown velvet suddenly disappeared. Stacey felt something on her shoulder. Just as if someone had laid a hand there. 'No offence meant, dear,' said Rosa Riedel, 'but I'm a ghost.'

Stacey jumped, and she almost felt scared again, but Rosa Riedel went on, 'Sort of a guardian ghost, if you like to put it that way.'

Stacey could feel Rosa stroking her hair, kindly and gently. 'See, ducky, doesn't matter if it's an angel or a ghost, does it?' Rosa whispered into her ear. 'It's the guardian bit that counts, right?'

Stacey had to agree. It was indeed the guardian bit that counted. She needed guarding against fear, and if there was a ghost prepared to do it for her, she had no objection. 'What do you look like, then, Rosa Riedel?' asked Stacey. 'Or don't you look like anything?'

'I looked like something once,' said Rosa Riedel. 'Just average, just normal, you know. A bit too fat. Well, a lot too fat, really. Flatfooted, too.' Rosa Riedel sighed. 'Stand about too long and I find my feet are killing me. Shooting pains right up my legs, I get.'

'What else?' asked Stacey.

'What else?' Rosa chuckled. 'Well, Franz, that was my husband, he thought I was pretty, but then again Minnie, that's my sister, she said I looked daft. And then again my brother Karl thought I just looked like other folk!'

'What colour are your eyes?' asked Stacey. 'And what's your nose like, and your ears?'

'Hard to describe yourself, isn't it?' sighed Rosa Riedel. 'But if you're so set on seeing me, I reckon it can be done for a minute or so.'

The sofa creaked again, the dent in the brown velvet was

back, and Rosa Riedel said, 'Now don't talk for a minute, ducky. I got to concentrate, see?'

First of all Stacey saw just the shimmering outline of Rosa Riedel, the way you see someone reflected in a window pane. Then Rosa Riedel became solider and more distinct. Stacey found herself sitting opposite a fat old woman with dark hair which had a few white hairs mixed into it. She wore round, nickel-framed glasses on her nose, which was round too, and rather small. Rosa Riedel also had sticking-out ears, a wide mouth, and fat cheeks. There was a pale brown wart on her left cheek. (This makes Rosa Riedel sound very ugly, but she wasn't. Put the round nose, the pouch-like cheeks, the jug ears and the wide mouth together, and they made up an extremely nice face.)

Stacey stared at Rosa Riedel until she went transparent again, like a shape reflected in a window, saying quietly, 'Sorry, ducky, can't keep it up any longer! It's a terrible strain materializing, you know.'

And then Rosa Riedel disappeared entirely. There was nothing left of her but her voice. 'Got a headache again now,' said the voice. 'Always gives me a headache, materializing does.'

Then Rosa Riedel chuckled softly. It sounded as if she were feeling shy. 'Well, ducky,' she chuckled, 'no beauty, am I?'

'I think you're nice,' said Stacey.

'Really and truly?'

'Really and truly,' said Stacey, and it was no lie. She thought Rosa Riedel was very nice indeed.

'That's all right then, ducky,' said Rosa Riedel, sounding pleased.

The bright green knitting suddenly jumped off the floor and hung in the air above the sofa. 'That purl's too loose,' said Rosa. The knitting needles clicked in the air. Stitches moved from the left-hand needle to the right-hand needle. The bright green ball of wool rolled towards the sofa. 'There,' said Rosa, 'now let's sit and have a chat till your mum and dad are home. But I'll have to be off when we hear them on the stairs. I only make contact in exceptional cases, see?'

Stacey was immensely pleased to think that Rosa Riedel counted her as an exceptional case.

6

Stacey's parents came home after midnight, together, because Dad had calmed down in the Western. When the film was over he went to the Zieselhuts'.

The Zieselhuts lived in a leafy green suburb. Their big living-room window looked out on the garden. If you were sitting by this window you could see the garden gate. Stacey's mum, who was sitting there, saw Dad come through the gate. She thought fast, and then cried, 'Good heavens, Bertie must be out of his mind! Here he comes, in spite of his lumbago!' (Mum had told the Zieselhuts he couldn't come with her because of a bad attack of lumbago.) Mum jumped up and ran to the front door, a picture of concern from her blonde chignon to the straps of her evening sandals. She flung the door open, hissing to Dad, who was about to put his finger on the bell, 'I said you had lumbago and couldn't move!'

'Want me to go away again?' inquired Dad.

'Don't be silly,' hissed Mum. 'They saw you through the window,' And indeed, along came Mrs Zieselhut, saying, 'Oh, Bertie, whatever are you thinking of, you dreadful man?' She was wagging her forefinger at him. Had she been asked in what way she was wagging this forefinger, she would certainly have said 'Roguishly'. Dad, however, did not ask Mrs Zieselhut any such question, but made a wry face, sighed, and said, 'Well, it's a bit better now!' And he limped towards the coat-stand. Mum helped him off with his coat. He limped into the living room. Mrs Zieselhut supported him. He limped over to a nice, soft leather armchair, but Mr Zieselhut cried, 'Oh, you'll find that one's too soft for lumbago,' and wouldn't let Dad sit in it. 'You'd never get up again!' And he fetched a hard wooden chair from the kitchen. 'This is the sort of chair you want with lumbago.' Mr Zieselhut had once had lumbago himself.

So Dad acted the part of a man with a bad back until well after midnight. He even asked one of the other guests to help him up when he had to go to the lavatory, making out he couldn't manage on his own. (He was limping all wrong, in fact, as if his left knee and not his back hurt him, but nobody noticed.)

Mum was grateful to Dad for not making her look silly in front of the Zieselhuts. And since she had been nice to him because of the other guests anyway, she went on being nice to him on the way home. She even said, 'I'll sort your socks out tomorrow.' And Dad said, 'What do socks matter, darling?' So then they laughed, and as they had just stopped at an intersection they kissed each other until the car behind them hooted, because the lights had turned green some time ago.

Dad was still limping when he got out of the car, he had grown so used to it.

Mum giggled when he limped upstairs ahead of her.

'You shouldn't laugh at a person's infirmities!' said Dad, and Mum said, 'Ssh, Bertie!' and went on giggling. The pair of them giggled their way upstairs. Then Mum unlocked the front door of the apartment and tried to walk into the hall. But she couldn't: she just couldn't. Something was barring her way. And at that moment the light in the passage outside, which automatically switched itself off after three minutes did so, and Mum couldn't even see what was in her way. 'Bertie, there's something here,' said Mum, not giggling any more.

'What d'you mean?' asked Dad, who was still having a fit of giggles. But suddenly the strange obstacle was gone. Mum stumbled into the apartment and switched on the hall light. Dad limped in after her.

'What was it?' he asked.

'I don't know,' said Mum. 'I tried to open the door and something stuck: it was awfully hard to open, and then I had a really peculiar feeling. Like being surrounded by warm, flabby rubber rings.'

'Darling, you've had a bit too much to drink,' said Dad, chuckling. He closed the front door, and at that very moment they heard the attic door slam shut on the floor above.

'Obvious!' said Dad, pointing to the open window in the hall. 'That window was open, you'd opened the front door, and some idiot left the attic door open again—it was a draught you felt.'

Mum and Dad found Stacey in the living room, sitting in Mum's TV chair, fast asleep. She was holding her bright green knitting.

Dad picked Stacey up. Mum took the knitting out of her hands. Dad carried Stacey into her own room. When he came back he said, 'She didn't even wake up when I undressed her. But she muttered something while I was tucking her in: "Sleep well, dear Rosa Riedel!" That's what she said. Who on earth is Rosa Riedel?'

Mum shrugged her shoulders. She knew no one by the name of Rosa Riedel, and at the moment she was fascinated by the bright green knitting anyway. She held it out to Dad. 'Look at that,' she said. 'What do you make of that, then?'

Dad looked at the knitting. 'It's a particularly ghastly shade of green,' he said.

'I don't mean that,' said Mum. 'I mean, what do you think of the way it's knitted?'

So Dad took a closer look at the knitting, and then he said, 'There's a small stretch of appalling work down at the bottom, but the rest of it, say about another fifty centimetres, that's perfect. Could have been machine-knitted!'

'Exactly!' said Mum. 'And all Stacey's knitting is appalling.'

'Well, she's just improved, then,' said Dad.

'This isn't the sort of thing you learn all of a sudden, Bertie, I assure you! It'd take years!'

'Oh, darling!' said Dad, yawning. 'You can see she has learned it! Or do you believe in brownies? It's not as if you'd really had all that much to drink!'

Mum did not believe in brownies, but nor did she believe Stacey could have learned to knit so beautifully so quickly. However, since she really had had a little too much to drink, and was also very tired, she decided not to think about it any more, but to ask Stacey in the morning. (By the morning, however, Mum had a headache, and she had forgotten all about the bright green knitting.)

7

Rosa Riedel told Stacey a great many things that Friday evening. Leaving out the unimportant parts, we get the following story. (You will see a few dots where I've left things out.)

'Why, no naturally I never reckoned on being a ghost, not while I was alive. I had an ordinary sort of life, ducky. I was a caretaker, went out cleaning for a few folk too, because you couldn't live off a caretaker's wages on their own then, any more than now. I didn't believe in ghosts either! I wasn't that struck on believing things anyway, I was more for thinking 'em out, see, getting to know things properly . . .

'Do I like it, being a ghost? Well, no, not really! Still, at least there's a bit of justice in it. After all, I reckon I'm the only working-class ghost in all Europe. All the rest are posh, see? Ghosts in castles, and mansions, and noblemen's family vaults and that. I could go along to their meetings, of course, but I don't fancy it. They're a nasty lot, you know. Not a single ghost among them that isn't a criminal. And I don't mean the crimes that got 'em into being ghosts, nor the things you read in books of ghost stories. I'm speaking of the way they lived when they was alive, and how they behaved to their workers and peasants, and the wars they started, and the way they laid into poor folk. Rosa Riedel's not mixing with the likes of them, I can tell you . . .

'Yes, well, a ghost needs to know a whole lot. I did fine at the start, oh yes! Floating about like a little cloud, going through the tiniest of keyholes. It's never been the same since 1945, though, when I was buried in the cellar of a bombed building. Underneath that rubble for two years, I was, squashed flat as a toad on the road. Well, it was a five-storey building. So no more floating. Got to get about on my own flat feet, same as any live person. No more going through keyholes neither. It's the lack of elasticity, you see . . .

'How did I get to be a ghost? Well, to tell you the truth, I'm not too sure. But I worked it out, more or less, and if you're going to see what I mean we'll have to go back a bit.

'Nobody wants to die, do they? But people's ways of dying are different, at that. My mother, for instance, she lived to be over eighty, she had four children and nine grandchildren. None of the children came to anything much, but she didn't mind. She reckoned the grandchildren would do better, some time. And eighty years, she said, that's long enough for one life, I did as I ought, everything's in order and I never was one for hanging about. So she died, and that was the end of her.

'Look at Miss Dostal, though, ever so ladylike, always fretting, when it's her turn to die she'll fret a bit more, and then that'll be that.

'Or take old Franz, him with the little dog, he doesn't like life. Never wanted a wife, never wanted children, if the sun's shining it's too hot for him, if it rains it's too wet, if it snows the snow's too white. He won't mind being dead and buried much, he never enjoyed life anyway.

'Can't say I enjoyed it that much myself! Real trouble, we had then. It was 1938, you see, when the Nazis came to power here in Austria, and the bad times got even worse. Oh, I could have wept with rage when all people could say was you had to take things as they come! When our landlady said "Heil Hitler!" to me, I was fit to burst with fury! And when I saw that Dostal woman, only she was just a girl then, sitting down in the yard, sewing swastikas on banners, I was fair seething! As for the way a lot of people talked about the Jews, saying that they didn't belong here because us Aryans was a superior race and ought not to mix with 'em, well, it was enough to take your breath away.

'Not that we had many Jews around here. Myself, I only knew Mr Fischer. He was a watchmaker, had a shop down on the corner. I cleaned for him every Thursday. He was a nice sort, never one for nit-picking. "I don't know what I'd do without you, Mrs Riedel," he always used to say.

'So I says to him, every Thursday around that time, "Mr Fischer," I says to him, "you don't want to stop here any longer! Those Nazis, they're bad news. Why don't you go to Switzerland?" I says to him. "Or America? Dr Goldberger's left, you know. And Mr Lederer the engineer's leaving next week, so I heard!" But Mr Fischer, he wouldn't listen to me. He'd done nothing wrong, he said. And he wasn't one of the rich sort of Jews, either. So there wasn't anything they could take from him. If he kept quiet, he said, he'd be all right. He was so simple, he couldn't rightly believe the terrible things that go on in the world.

'"A clear conscience is a soft pillow," he used to say. And come to that, leaving wasn't so easy if you didn't have money. They only wanted rich Jews in Switzerland, and if you were going to America you needed someone to vouch for you as a Jewish emigrant to the government there, and where would Mr Fischer have found somebody to vouch for him?

'So he stayed put, and when that Nazi riffraff painted DIRTY JEW on his shop windows by night he washed it off again next morning. And when folk cut him dead in the street, he looked the other way and didn't say anything. And when that fool Fred Dostal, ever-so-refined Miss Dostal's brother, spat at him, he made out he hadn't noticed.

'So then, just as I was on my way home from a cleaning job, with a lady called Beierl it was, and I was passing Mr Fischer's shop, only unfortunately on the other side of the street, I saw these two stormtroopers in their brown uniforms, with their swastika armbands and all, hauling Mr Fischer out of his shop and dragging him to the corner. Because there was three red arrows painted on the pavement. That was the symbol of our party you see, the Socialist party. Our people had painted them on the pavement by night, so's the Nazis would realize we were still around, and we weren't knuckling under so easy.

'Anyway, these two stormtroopers dragged Mr Fischer over to our arrows. There was a crowd of people on the corner. The stormtroopers gave Mr Fischer a toothbrush, and one of them kicked him, so Mr Fischer fell over, and a few of the crowd laughed. The stormtroopers hauled Mr Fischer up again and pointed to the arrows and shouted, "Clean that off, dirty Jew!"

'Some of the folk standing around Mr Fischer and the stormtroopers was Nazis, but there were some among them I knew, and they were no Nazis, but did they go to help Mr Fischer? Not them. Then I felt so furious, oh, I was really wild, I just saw red! I wanted to cross the road and help him, and tell those that wasn't Nazis we had to do something about it, this kind of thing wouldn't do. So I did cross the road, without looking.

'Well, the tram couldn't stop quick enough. "Mr Fischer!" I called. "I'm just coming, Mr Fischer!" And I was going to say, "Help him, why don't you?" but I never got it out.

'You see how it was, ducky? That tram ran me over just as I was, all full of rage and anger, but hopeful too, hopeful we could still do something to help Mr Fischer, at least. So what I reckon is: if a person's got something as urgent to do as I had then, if a person's as furious as I was, then they can't die properly because they're not at peace.

'It was terrible, I can tell you. There I lay, dead, watching poor old Mr Fischer scrub away at the three arrows with that toothbrush. The ambulance came and they put me on a stretcher. "Nothing I can do," says the doctor. And they spread a big sheet of brown paper over me. Covered my head too, they did.

'They're crazy, I thought. It's just that I can't talk. Can't move either. But I'm alive right enough! Got to get up and go and help Mr Fischer. Got to tell those people it's all wrong, it's a crime!

'But try as I might, I couldn't move. Nor talk either. I could feel it all though. Them putting me in a coffin, and shoving me into a hearse, and unloading me at the chapel in the cemetery, I felt the whole thing!

'So they put me in the chapel, and my funeral service began, with the clergyman carrying on and a crowd of people there. There was wreaths on my coffin, and bunches of flowers, and my husband, that I'd never seen cry in his life, he was crying. And suddenly there was Mrs Berger and old Mrs Huber beside my coffin, talking in whispers, saying what terrible times these were. "Poor Rosa Riedel," they were saying, "poor Rosa run over, and poor Mr Fischer lying there at home, that terrible thing giving him a stroke so's he can't ever move again!" Paralyzed down one side they said he was, and nobody to look after him. So I says to myself: Rosa, you've got to go and see Mr Fischer! Rosa, Mr Fischer needs you! Rosa, I says to myself, you just get out of this stupid box this minute, Rosa!

'It worked, too. I got up and climbed out of that coffin. Won't they just be surprised, I thought. But they weren't surprised. They didn't see me at all. My dead body stayed there in the coffin, you see. That had me upset at first. But then I thought it over, and I said to myself: Well, in times like these, it's no bad thing to be invisible.

'But I did want to find out if I could be heard or not. So I went over to our landlady, who was standing near the chapel door along with Mrs Dostal, telling her, "Say what you like about Mrs Riedel, you have to give her one thing: I'll never find a better cleaning lady!" Then I whispered into our landlady's left ear, "Well, I wouldn't have gone on cleaning for you anyway, I don't go cleaning for Nazis, let 'em clean up after their own dirty selves!"

'Our landlady went white as a sheet and started shaking all over. "Dear me, whatever is the matter?" says Mrs Dostal to her. "Are you feeling indisposed?" (This Mrs Dostal was Miss Dostal's mother, see, and just as refined and posh as her daughter.) So I moved over to Mrs Dostal's left ear, and I said, "Reckon you'll be feeling indisposed yourself before too long, you old humbug, and if I see that daughter of yours down in the yard sewing swastikas on banners any more, I'll be at your bedside every night pinching you black and blue!"

'Then Mrs Dostal and our landlady fainted dead away, and while the clergyman was saying the last of his stuff over my body, the undertaker's men took the pair of them out into the fresh air and laid them on a cemetery seat and fanned 'em. And I said to myself, "Rosa Riedel," I said, "you're a little bit of a chance for the future now. Rosa, you just get down to work!"'

8

Next morning Stacey felt as if she hadn't had enough sleep, but perfectly cheerful and happy. She even ate some breakfast, something she usually did only on days when there was no school. However, Mum didn't notice, because she had not had a good night herself: also she had her headache.

Stacey left the apartment three minutes earlier than usual. She stole up the stairs to the attic, opened the attic door just a crack, and asked the beat-up old velvet sofa, 'Are you still asleep, Rosa?'

'Just this minute woke up,' said Rosa Riedel, yawning. 'I always wake up about now. It's when Mrs Berger turns her radio on. I can hear everything it plays!'

'See you after lunch, then, Rosa dear,' said Stacey, and she closed the door again and ran downstairs.

Tina was waiting outside the building, as usual. They walked down the street. 'What are you going to wear this afternoon?' Tina asked. 'My mum wants me to wear my pink dress, but I don't like it. I'd rather go in jeans. It's not such a posh party as all that!'

'I'm not going,' said Stacey. 'I've got to do something else.'

'Not going?' Tina goggled at her. 'You crazy? What are you going to do then! You were looking forward to Tommy's birthday party so much!'

Stacey had indeed been looking forward to Tommy's birthday party, but Rosa Riedel was more important now. And of course Stacey couldn't tell Tina the truth. Rosa Riedel didn't want her to, and Stacey didn't want to anyway. Rosa Riedel was all hers. She didn't want to share her with anyone else.

'What are you going to do?' Tina pressed her.

Stacey did not like lying. I'll stick to the truth as far as possible, she thought. 'Well, I met this old lady,' she said.

'So?' said Tina.

'So I promised to go for a walk with her.'

'Are you daft?' asked Tina. 'If you really want to hang around with some old lady, you can do it another time!'

'No, it has to be today!'

'And why does it have to be today, Princess Anastasia?' inquired Tina, looking fierce.

'It just does,' said Stacey. 'Anyway, it's none of your business!'

'Peculiar,' said Tina crossly. 'Very peculiar! Princess Anastasia would rather hang round with an old woman than go to a birthday party, would she?'

Stacey didn't answer.

'I know why, too!' Tina went on. 'It's because Tommy didn't ask darling Michael, that's why!' And Tina rolled her eyes and stretched her mouth into a huge grin intended to convey great disgust.

Tina and Stacey walked to school in silence. At the school gates, Tina said, 'I tell you one thing, if you don't come to that party today you're not my friend any more. We'll be enemies for ever!'

'Don't be silly,' said Stacey.

Tina put her tongue out and marched off to the classroom.

The teachers were not pleased with Stacey that morning, either. The German teacher said, 'Do stop daydreaming, Stacey!' five times during the first period. Second period was even worse. The maths teacher made Stacey come to the board and add up $\frac{1}{4}$ and $\frac{1}{8}$ and $\frac{1}{12}$. Naturally Stacey could do simple sums like that all right; indeed, she was very good at arithmetic. But this morning she kept on thinking of Rosa Riedel, and Mr Fischer, and Rosa's funeral, until she was no longer sure if four quarters really did make up one whole, and it seemed perfectly possible that one-eighth might be twice as much as one-quarter. In the end she worked out that the sum came to five. The maths teacher looked at her sadly, and Tina looked at her with a grin, nudged the girl sitting in front of her and whispered, 'Fancy her getting top marks in maths!'

Stacey tried the sum again, and this time she made the result one-eighth. The maths teacher was looking at her with concern now. 'What's the matter, Stacey?' he asked. 'Aren't you feeling very well? Are you sick?' Tina turned to the boy sitting behind her and whispered, 'If one of us gets a sum wrong, we're just stupid! But of course if Princess Anastasia says something stupid, she has to be sick!' The boy sitting behind her nodded, and whispered, 'Nobody could be so sick they'd get a daft result like that!'

The maths teacher sent Stacey back to her desk and did the sum himself. Stacey sat down beside Tina again. 'Well, Miss Anastasia,' Tina hissed at her. 'One of our little princess's off days, is it?' Then Tina pushed Stacey's ballpoint pen and eraser over from the middle of the desk to Stacey's side of it, saying nastily, 'I need a bit of room too, you know!'

Stacey spent the rest of the maths lesson drawing tiny little red arrows in groups of three on the last page of her rough book. Now and then she looked out of the window and smiled.

At break she went to look at the aquarium with Michael, The aquarium was on the top floor, by the staircase. Michael and Stacey tried to count the fishes and couldn't, because they all looked the same, and they wouldn't keep still, but kept swimming busily around. Tina followed them up. She kept her distance and stood there eating an enormous cheese and sausage sandwich, watching them. When Tommy came upstairs to look at the aquarium too, she said, 'Don't disturb love's young dream, will you, Tommy?'

'She's an idiot!' Stacey told Michael.

'I thought you were friends with her,' said Michael.

Stacey did not reply, because she was looking at Tina, who was now talking quietly to Tommy. Stacey knew exactly what Tina was telling Tommy: Stacey wasn't coming to his birthday party because Michael hadn't been invited. Tommy came over to the aquarium too, planted himself in front of Stacey and asked, 'Is that right, then?'

'Is what right?' asked Stacey, making out she had no idea.

'Tina says you're not coming to my party because you'd rather hang around with some old lady!'

Stacey just nodded. Tommy shrugged his shoulders, muttering, 'Well, it's your choice?' and went back to Tina.

Michael looked at Stacey and said, 'Tina told me the only reason you weren't going was because I won't be there.'

'That's silly,' said Stacey, 'I mean, I'm sorry he didn't invite you, but I'd have gone all the same. Only—well, I really am going out with an old lady!'

'Can I come too?' asked Michael. 'It might be more fun with three.'

'No, sorry.' Stacey hesitated briefly, not wishing to upset Michael too. 'Some other time, maybe, Michael. But honestly, you can't today. You see, this old lady's very timid—imagine, she hasn't been out of the house for thirty years . . . ' Stacey fell silent. She hadn't really meant to tell Michael so much.

Michael laughed. 'Come off it, Stacey! You're making it up!' And he added, quickly, 'Not that I mind you telling me stories, honest!'

'I'm not telling stories!' snapped Stacey, turning and running downstairs. The bell was just ringing for the end of break. Stacey sat down at her desk. She stayed there till school finished at mid-day. She took no notice of Tina's cross glances: she drew arrows, and hearts with arrows through them, and made the letters R.R. into a monogram. She was asked seven questions and was unable to give seven answers, because she hadn't heard the questions. Once, her pen rolled off the desk, and Tina picked it up. (Which was surely an offer to cease hostilities, or at the very least call a truce.) Stacey never even noticed.

When she got home from school, Mum was in the kitchen ironing her flowered blue dress. 'For the party,' she explained.

Stacey decided to lie to Mum. It was a pity, but she would have to. She could hardly say, 'Mum, I'm not going to the party, because I met a ghost yesterday evening, my guardian ghost, and this ghost has got rather shy of people over the last ten years, so I'm going to take her out for a little walk this afternoon. You see, the ghost said she thought she might venture out if I was with her.'

Mum would have dropped the iron if Stacey had said that or anything like it. Very likely she would not have been satisfied with this amount of information either, she would have gone asking questions, and then Stacey would have had to tell her everything. And Mum would have explained that she was just dreaming yesterday evening, and there were no such things as ghosts, and a big girl like Stacey shouldn't believe such nonsense. There was one other possibility, of course: Stacey could have asked Rosa Riedel to come down from the attic, and Rosa Riedel could have talked to Mum. If Rosa made a bit of an effort she could have materialized too. Then Mum would have just had to believe in her. But Stacey was sure Rosa Riedel wouldn't like the idea. 'I only make contact in exceptional cases,' that was what she'd told Stacey. Stacey didn't like the idea either. Rosa Riedel was not a family ghost, was she? She was all Stacey's.

So Stacey simply gave Mum and the flowered blue dress a friendly nod, saying, 'Mum, listen, I'm leaving a bit early to meet Tina and a few of the others first. We're—er—we're going to buy Tommy a bunch of flowers.'

'Flowers for a boy?' asked Mum. Well, Stacey explained, she didn't really mean flowers. A cactus, that was what they were going to buy Tommy. Tommy collected cacti. Mum said a nice-looking cactus cost a lot of money if it was any size. 'I tell you what,' said Mum, generously, 'I'll give you our globe cactus for Tommy!' Stacey tried to look pleased, and succeeded.

9

So at about two o'clock, carrying a globe cactus wrapped in white tissue paper and tied up with a sky-blue bow, Stacey crept up to the attic. She unwrapped the cactus and put it down near the velvet sofa. Rosa Riedel was pleased. She liked a nice cactus.

'Is there anything else you could do with?' asked Stacey.

'Well, if it's not too much trouble, dear,' said Rosa Riedel, 'I wouldn't mind an alarm clock, or any other sort, come to that. I never know what the time is, see, not unless Mrs Berger has her radio on.'

Stacey promised Rosa an alarm clock and a little transistor radio. She decided to bring Rosa Riedel a pillow and a blanket too, but she said nothing about that. She might find a small bedside rug as well. She wanted Rosa to be nice and comfortable.

Just as she was about to leave the attic Stacey heard steps on the stairs. She hid behind a pile of planks standing near the sofa.

Miss Dostal came in with a basket of washing. She went to the washing line slung across the attic and started hanging out her things. She did it very slowly. She pulled every piece of washing into shape first, and shook it out, and then pegged it to the line. It was very dusty behind the planks. Stacey struggled desperately against a tickle in her nose which was getting worse and worse. Miss Dostal was just taking a blue towel with pink roses on it out of her washing basket and shaking it when Stacey sneezed out loud.

'Oh, may goodness me!' cried Miss Dostal, and she dropped the towel, pressing both hands to her left breast, over her heart. Then she ran to the attic door as fast as she could, stumbled down the stairs, and rang the doorbell of Stacey's apartment, still wailing, 'Oh, may word, whet a shock Ay hev hed!'

Rosa Riedel took Stacey's hand and pulled her out from behind the pile of planks. 'Just you keep calm, ducky!' she whispered. 'All in the day's work to a ghost, this sort of thing! Leave it to me! I'm going down now to distract your mum's attention!'

'How?' whispered Stacey, putting two fingers in her mouth and biting their nails.

'You wait there till the coast's clear,' said Rosa Riedel. 'Till that Miss Dostal's inside your apartment, I mean. Then you can nip downstairs and we'll meet by the front door.'

Stacey went on biting her nails. Rosa Riedel put a hand on her shoulder and propelled her gently towards the attic door. Down below, Stacey's mother was just opening the door of their apartment. 'Hello, Miss Dostal, what's the matter?' she asked.

'Ay hev hed a shock!' wailed Miss Dostal. 'Up in thet ettic! Ay heard someone go Hay-tishoo!'

'You heard someone sneezing?' asked Stacey's mother, bewildered. 'Who?'

'Right, here goes!' whispered Rosa Riedel. Stacey could feel Rosa's soft warmth squeezing past her. She heard Miss Dostal wailing, 'Ay do not know who! But Ay swear there is someone in thet ettic! Haiding in the corner, behaind the planks! Ooh, Ay was never so fraightened in may laife! We must call the police!' There was a moment's silence, and then Miss Dostal began giggling. Quietly at first, then louder and louder, until finally she was squealing like a piglet.

Feeling curious, Stacey ventured a couple of steps down

the stairs and leaned over the banisters. She saw a horrified Mum, and she saw Miss Dostal. Miss Dostal was hopping about and flinging herself around and waving her arms as if she were trying to do a Scottish reel.

'Miss Dostal, please!' Stacey's mum put both hands on Miss Dostal's shoulders. 'Do calm down, for goodness' sake!'

'Ooh, Ay say, it tickles!' squealed Miss Dostal. 'Ay em ever so ticklish! It tickles all over!' And she went on hopping and waving and giggling.

'You poor creature,' said Mum in a soothing tone, like a nurse. 'Come along in, now, and calm down!' She took Miss Dostal into the apartment and closed the door. The giggling and squealing was not so loud now. Stacey made her way downstairs. As she passed the door, she heard Miss Dostal saying, 'Ay must tell the police—teehee—of the sneeze in the ettic.'

Stacey ran downstairs. She stood by the front door of the building, panting, put her two fingers back in her mouth and bit the nails. 'There we are, then!' said Rosa Riedel, as she bit off the first piece of nail.

They left the building. 'Mum thinks Miss Dostal's off her head,' said Stacey.

'Too bad,' said Rosa Riedel, chuckling.

'What do you want to do, then, Rosa?' asked Stacey, and suddenly looked down at the ground, embarrassed because a lady who had been walking behind them passed at this moment, looking at her curiously. It isn't every day you come across a child who looks perfectly normal but is talking to herself.

'Oh, just walk about a bit for a start,' said Rosa, 'so's I can get used to all the crowds and the streets and the cars again, see?'

Stacey held hands with Rosa whenever they came to a

street corner: Rosa would never have ventured over the road on her own. 'Oh, what a nasty stink!' complained Rosa. 'Like being in a petrol can, it is! Let's go to a park. My feet are killing me too.'

Stacey took Rosa Riedel to the nearest park. It was a small and not very attractive park, but Rosa liked it all the same. 'Smells of spring,' she said. They sat down on a seat by the children's playground.

'Didn't you ever get bored,' asked Stacey, 'spending thirty years in the same building?'

'No, ducky,' said Rosa Riedel, 'not so's you'd notice. I moved around the building, you see, there isn't an apartment in the place I don't know back to front. And sometimes I went out in the yard in summer when the sun was shining.'

'If I could be invisible like that,' said Stacey, dreamily, 'I'd want to go everywhere. I could fly to Mexico without a ticket. I could get into important people's houses. I could sit on stage at the theatre—'

'Well, I tell you what it is, ducky,' said Rosa Riedel, 'I've had enough of that lot. I had a busy time in the war, you know, quite a strain it was, never a moment's rest. Pinching Nazi officials, scaring Hitler Youth lads, turning meetings of the Nazi Women's Fellowship upside down, upsetting ceremonies in honour of Hitler, and those were just the details. Main job I had to do was seeing there was a bit of justice in the building. I used to share jam and bacon and eggs about the place. Sometimes I got things wrong. For instance, there was the landlady's red felt boots I took off of her, seeing as she had three pairs of boots anyway. I put 'em in at Mrs Wokurka's door. But Mrs Wokurka couldn't wear them, because the landlady would have known her boots right away. So she sold them on the black market, for four kilos of flour. And as luck would have it, the landlady went to the pictures, to see a film starring Marika Rokk, and a woman sat down beside her—wearing her own boots! Oh, what a fuss there was! If I hadn't happened to be in the cinema too, because I used to be ever so keen on Marika Rokk—well, I don't hardly like to think what might have happened. The landlady wanted to drag the lady wearing the boots off to the police. But I looked sharp and jumped on the landlady's back, clung there like a heavy sack, all my weight on her, and I whispered in her ear, "And how are you going to explain to the police where you got the boots then?" Because I knew she'd got those boots on the black market herself. So she went white as a sheet, and just to make sure she didn't do anything to hurt the lady in her boots I whispered, "And if you go to the police now, you old fright, I'll stay on your back, and when we get to the police station I'll tell them your grandson's always trying to tune into the forbidden English wavelength on the radio!" I never would have done it, stands to reason. Hans, that was the landlady's grandson, he was the only decent person in that whole family. It worked, though. The landlady apologized to the other lady, and said it was all a mistake. She didn't want to see the film any more, so she left the cinema, and I had her seat.'

Stacey laughed. Rosa Riedel sighed. 'Sounds funny, yes, but it wasn't funny at the time.'

'What else did you do in those days?' asked Stacey.

'Well, I spent a lot of time down in the cellar,' Rosa said. 'When there were air raids. The people were ever so scared down there, specially the little kids. Your friend Tina's father, he was just a little lad then, he was so scared he couldn't move when the planes flew over and the bombs went off. I used to sit beside him and give him a hug and tell him it'd be all right, I was sure it'd be all right, though I wasn't so sure really, not so sure at all. And when it got so bad the whole cellar shook and people started praying I told him stories. Stories about wonderful countries where sausages and ham and spring chickens flew about in the air, and raspberry cordial came out of the taps—a piece of ham and a bar of chocolate was more of a fairy-tale to the children in those days than dwarves and enchanted princesses and that, you see.'

A woman came over to the seat holding a little boy's hand. Rosa stopped talking. The woman sat down on the seat. The little boy stood there kicking the gravel. 'Want to go on the swings!' he said.

'Now stop that kicking,' said the woman. 'It won't do your shoes any good!' The little boy started making for the playground, but the woman stopped him. 'Eat your sandwich first!' she said. She picked the little boy up, put him on the seat, took a large sandwich out of her basket and handed it to him. 'And you don't get down until you've eaten that, Arnim!' Little Arnim clutched the large sandwich, looked at it, and didn't bite it. The woman looked grimly ahead of her, saying, 'Come along, Arnim, eat up or I shall be cross with you!' every few moments, in a monotonous way. Arnim started crying but failed to start eating. Stacey decided to get up and walk off. She did not like the woman. Rosa Riedel whispered, 'Wait by the playground. I'm about to lend a hand here.'

Stacey sat down on an empty swing and looked back at the seat, waiting for Rosa to lend a hand.

Little Arnim was crying so hard now that the tears fell on his sandwich. The woman took it away from him, held it right in front of his mouth and said, 'Go on, eat it!' And as Arnim still didn't eat it, she smacked the back of his head. She was going to smack him again, but she found that she couldn't. Rosa pushed the smacking hand down on the arm of the seat, and pushed the sandwich-holding hand away from Arnim. Stacey saw the woman struggling, but Rosa was stronger. She forced the hand holding the sandwich towards the woman's own mouth, until the thick bread was touching her thin lips. And a deep, gentle voice could be heard all the way to Stacey's swing, saying, 'Go on, dear, eat up!' The woman did not want to eat up any more than Arnim had. But she did want to scream with fright, and as she opened her mouth to scream Rosa stuffed a corner of the sandwich into it. The woman choked, and swallowed, and Rosa went on cramming the sandwich into her mouth, bit by bit, until it was all inside. Then the deep, gentle voice said, 'Good girl, good girl, you can get up now!' The woman was looking very peculiar. She had tears in her eyes and her cheeks were stuffed with the sandwich. She gulped and swallowed, she grabbed hold of Arnim and her basket, she jumped up and ran for the park gates as if seven fierce hounds were chasing her.

Rosa came over to the swing. 'That'll teach her to bully little boys!' she said.

Watching the woman go, Stacey saw her pick Arnim up and run on— and then, suddenly, she felt something damp on her leg. Turning, she saw that the damp thing was a large dog's muzzle, belonging to a huge St. Bernard. Before Stacey could even start trembling, everything around her went very warm. Rosa Riedel was surrounding her like a big soft eiderdown, murmuring, 'There now, Rosa's here, dear. He's a nice dog, look! Wagging his tail and his ears, see? Nasty dogs lay their ears back and their tails go all stiff!'

Stacey knew very well that you could tell a nice dog by the way he wagged his ears and his tail, but it had never helped her get over her fear of dogs.

'I'll just see if he likes to be patted,' Rosa whispered. 'Some dogs don't.' The St. Bernard didn't mind being patted. He lay down on the ground and rolled, legs in the air, and let Rosa scratch his stomach. He was slavering with pleasure. He also gave happy little yelps.

The master of the St. Bernard was leaning against a tree. He whistled for his dog, and when the dog didn't get up and run to the tree he called, 'Ajax! Ajax!' And when the dog still didn't come, the man went over to him. 'What's the matter, Ajax?' he said. 'Is that any way for a grown dog to behave? Have you got fleas, or what?'

Bending down, he examined the dog's stomach. 'Oh, good heavens!' he said to Stacey. 'There's something wrong with him, poor fellow! Look at that—he's having muscular spasms!' Indeed, such a notion might well occur to anyone who didn't know that a kind, invisible, strong hand was scratching the dog's stomach, stroking it so that the hair of its coat moved this way and that with the movement of the hand.

'I'll have to call a vet,' said the man. 'Perhaps he's eaten something poisonous. Look, there's saliva running out of his mouth!'

'Stop it, Rosa!' whispered Stacey. The man didn't notice: he was too worried about his 'sick' dog. Rosa stopped stroking. The dog turned on his side and got up. 'False alarm!' said the man. 'Thank goodness for that!' The dog snuffled around a bit, licked the air three times (just where Rosa's hand was) and then ran over to the tree and lifted a leg. The man followed him.

'See how it is?' sighed Rosa. 'Can't even stroke a dog in peace, not if you're a ghost! There's always trouble when you go out.'

Stacey and Rosa left the park. The streets were very crowded now, and people kept treading on Rosa's flat feet or thumping her in the stomach. And when they turned into a quiet side street where there were hardly any cars or people, a large ball hit Rosa right in the chest.

'Watch what you're doing, you fool!' Rosa snapped at the boy who had thrown the ball. The boy who had thrown the ball, and the boy who had been going to catch it, were rooted to the spot. It was not so much hearing what Rosa said as the fact that the ball suddenly stopped halfway through the air and then bounced back at the boy who had thrown it. When Stacey and Rosa turned the next corner, the two boys were still standing there, transfixed, their ball rolling slowly down the street.

'I might have known it,' sighed Rosa. 'An old ghost like me should stay at home. The street's no place for an old ghost like me.'

Stacey thought it was still too soon to go home. Birthday parties usually last longer than two hours. Stacey suggested going to the cinema. Stacey asked if Rosa would like to see the lion cubs in the zoo, or go for a ride on the new underground. Or look in shop windows. Rosa Riedel didn't want to do any of those things. She said she didn't need to go to the cinema: she watched television almost every evening, usually at Miss Dostal's because she had the best colour telly, but when Miss Dostal was watching programmes Rosa didn't like, she went round to old Mrs Berger's to watch her telly instead.

Nor was Rosa interested in the lion cubs: she told Stacey that a tabby cat came up to the attic every day anyway, and a cat was all she needed.

She was not keen on the underground either, nor did she want to look in shop windows. She knew more than enough about their contents from the ads on TV, and clothes and food and drink meant nothing to her anyway. A ghost has no use for such things. All Rosa Riedel wanted to do was go back to her attic for an afternoon nap. So Stacey walked home with her.

At the door of the building, Rosa said, 'Reckon I won't be leaving home again in a hurry!' On the first floor, she said, 'No point in going out, far's I can see. My feet hurt, my innards hurt and my head hurts too.' On the second floor, she said, 'Well thanks very much for taking me, ducky! Tata, then! Just pop up and see me when you feel like it!'

Stacey waited for the attic door to swing open, squealing, and then close again, and wondered how to explain her early return home to Mum. Being unable to think of any good explanation, she rang Mrs Berger's bell. Mrs Berger was always pleased to see Stacey.

Today was no exception. Mrs Berger gave Stacey raspberry juice and biscuits, and told her, in great excitement, that refined Miss Dostal had had a 'seizure'. First she thought there was a burglar in the attic, then she thought somebody was tickling her. Terrible, it had been! Stacey pretended to be much surprised. Then she asked Mrs Berger, in a casual way, as if she wasn't specially interested, 'Mrs Berger, did you ever know somebody called Rosa Riedel?'

Mrs Berger sat down at the table opposite Stacey.

'Why, of course I knew Rosa,' she said. 'Everybody knew Rosa. Ah, dear me, Rosa Riedel! Who's been telling you about her, then?'

Stacey told a lie. 'Miss Dostal.'

'Well, don't you go believing her!' said Mrs Berger. 'She'll have said no good of Rosa, I'll be bound! Rosa was all right, though, believe you me! She was caretaker of the building over the yard, where Tina lives. She was always helping people out. I don't know what I'd have done without Rosa when my children were little and I had to go to work! When they were sick, Rosa used to keep an eye on them, and she'd go shopping for me. And she never asked any money for it. "You've nothing to spare yourself," she used to say.' Mrs Berger shook her head sadly. 'And then she goes and walks into a tram! Right slap into a tram! To this day, I can't see how she came to do it.'

'It was because she saw what the Nazi stormtroopers were doing to Mr Fischer,' said Stacey, and immediately wished she had kept her mouth shut.

'Whatever do you know about stormtroopers, and Mr Fischer?' Mrs Berger was looking surprised.

'Er—Miss Dostal—'stammered Stacey, but Mrs Berger interrupted her. 'Don't you go telling me that Dostal woman told you about Fischer! Not her, she didn't!'

'Well, then it must have been Granny Wokurka,' lied Stacey. This satisfied Mrs Berger. 'That's more like it,' she said. 'Yes, they were neighbours. And friends. I was friends with them too, in a way. I often used to talk to Mrs Wokurka about Rosa, when we were sheltering down in the cellars during the war. I never stayed in this building, you see, not when the air raid warnings went, I always went over to Mrs Wokurka's. I thought their cellar was safer, and the children didn't kick up so much row there.' Mrs Berger smiled. 'And then it was there the bombs fell, after all!'

'Were you in that cellar at the time?' asked Stacey. Mrs Berger nodded. 'That was no fun, I can tell you! But we all managed to get out before the building came down. It didn't collapse completely until the last person was up the cellar stairs and out. Like a real miracle, it was, everybody said so at the time!'

Stacey looked out of the window and across the yard, to the building where Tina and Granny Wokurka lived, and where Rosa Riedel used to live herself.

'The whole place went,' Mrs Berger was going on. 'Nothing left of it but a great heap of rubble. Then, in '48, they cleared the rubble away and put a new building up.'

Mrs Berger got up and went to the window. 'Ah, dear me, Rosa Riedel!' she said, smiling. 'You'd have liked her, Stacey, believe you me!'

'Oh, I do,' said Stacey earnestly. 'I do believe you.'

10

Hard as Stacey tried to persuade Rosa Riedel to go out again, Rosa would not. 'An old ghost like me belongs at home!' she said stubbornly. Rosa was all for regularity and routine. 'An old ghost like me needs a bit of order,' she said firmly. She made out a timetable for Stacey. It went like this: 7.30 to 7.45 a.m., Stacey visits Rosa's attic. 2.10 to 3.30 or 4.30 p.m., Stacey visits Rosa's attic again. 7.30 to 10.00 p.m., Rosa visits Stacey's apartment.

In case they needed each other urgently outside these visiting times, they arranged a series of signals. There was an old iron flue grating on the wall behind Stacey's bed. If Stacey hit the flue with the hammer from her fretwork set, Rosa could hear it quite clearly in the attic above. They agreed on two signals. One knock meant: I don't absolutely have to see you, but it would be nice if you could come down. Two knocks meant: I need you urgently! (Of course the signals worked the other way around as well: if Rosa hit the flue grating up in the attic, Stacey could hear it down in her own room.)

When Rosa and Stacey had been friends for three weeks, Stacey came home from school one day and noticed that Mum was not the same as usual. She just said, 'Hi,' rather grumpily when Stacey opened the front door. She put a plate of pancakes and a bowl of cherry jam on the kitchen table without a word, and then washed dishes.

Stacey sat down at the kitchen table, helped herself to cherry jam, ate the pancakes, and waited for Mum to ask how school had been, how was Tina today, did Stacey have much homework and was Michael's cold better? But Mum asked none of these questions.

'We got our English test back,' said Stacey. Mum washed some plates and made no comment.

'I got A,' said Stacey. Mum washed some cups and didn't say a word.

Stacey repeated it. 'I got A!' As Mum still did not answer, she went on. 'I was the only person with an A! Twelve people got D. Tina was one of them. The rest were all Cs, and a couple of Bs!' Surely Mum must say something nice now, offer congratulations . . . well done, dear, or something! Mum picked up the teacloth and dried the cups and plates. Stacey wondered if she'd had a quarrel with Dad, and decided not. Dad had gone to the office in a perfectly good temper that morning, and Stacey was sure he hadn't been home since then. Anyway, Mum was looking cross. After a quarrel with Dad she looked miserable and sick.

'What's the matter, Mum?' asked Stacey.

Mum put the teacloth down and came over to the table. She sat down opposite Stacey. 'I am sorry to say I've found out that you're systematically telling me lies!' she said. In her alarm, Stacey swallowed three cherry-stones. 'But—but I'm not, Mum!' she said feebly.

'Oh yes, you are,' said Mum. 'You are telling me lies, and I'm worried because I don't know why!'

Mum had happened to meet Tommy's mother in the supermarket, and Tommy's mother had told her about the birthday party, and the seven dozen empty Coca-Cola bottles and the grilled sausages and the tombola prizes, and had said she was sorry Stacey couldn't come. And on her way home from the supermarket, Mum had gone into the dairy, where she met old Mrs Wokurka, from whom she learned that Stacey and Tina had not been friends for over three weeks. Old Mrs Wokurka had told Mum Tina was very upset, and sat around at home every afternoon moping because of Stacey.

'So where do you go in the afternoons?' asked Mum. 'Why say you're going to Tina's? If you've made friends with some other girl, surely you could tell me?'

Stacey said nothing.

'It makes me think all sorts of awful things!' said Mum. 'What *do* you do in the afternoons—and why do you have to keep it quiet?'

'I'm not doing anything awful,' said Stacey.

'Then you can tell me about it,' cried Mum.

'No,' said Stacey.

Here Mum really lost her temper. Evidently she'd thought Stacey would tell her the truth about her afternoons if she spoke to her seriously and kindly. She hadn't expected Stacey just to say no.

'Well, you're not going out any more until you tell me where it is you go,' said Mum.

'Honestly, I'm not doing anything wrong,' said Stacey, starting to cry. Through her sobs, she said it was horrible for mothers to keep wanting to know absolutely everything about their children.

'I've a right to a private life of my own,' she cried. 'You tell lies yourself!' she cried. 'You go telling the Zieselhuts Dad's got lumbago!'

Mum said that was quite different. It was all right not to tell the Zieselhuts the exact truth. She wouldn't mind Stacey herself not telling Tina the truth now and then. But there had to be a 'basis of trust' between parents and children in a family, said Mum.

'Right, then we've got a basis of trust if I don't tell you something, but you still believe I'm not doing anything wrong!' sobbed Stacey. 'Only you don't trust me, do you? You think I'm doing something bad!'

Stacey fell silent and went on sobbing quietly. Mum was

impressed. She said, 'But Stacey—' twice, and could get no farther.

Stacey took a deep breath, and let fly. 'So what *do* you think I'm up to, then? You think I break into the supermarket every afternoon? You think I sell pot on the corner of the street? You think I let old men pet me in doorways?'

Mum's eyes and mouth flew open in horror. Obviously she had never suspected any of these frightful things. 'What on earth's got into you?' she cried. 'I'd never believe you'd do anything like that!'

'Then you're just very, very curious,' said Stacey.

'No, I'm not. Really I'm not,' Mum defended herself. She thought for a moment, and then added, hesitantly, 'I'm sure it's not just curiosity. I worry! And if you're not going to tell me where you go, then you might at least tell me why you can't tell me!'

Stacey pushed the last of her pancake around her plate. Could she tell Mum about Rosa after all? Rosa hadn't actually forbidden her to! She'd only said there was no point in it, because grown-ups get into a state when obliged to believe in ghosts. Grown-ups, said Rosa, would sooner believe in flying saucers or fork-bending or little green men from Mars.

Stacey looked thoughtfully at Mum. Perhaps Mum was different? Mum seemed neither fragile nor unimaginative.

She was almost prepared to tell Mum about Rosa Riedel when Mum said, 'Lies like that rattle me, dear, you see!'

If 'lies like that' rattled Mum, then what would the existence of Rosa do to her? No, Mum couldn't be expected to take Rosa!

Stacey decided to try a half truth. Half truths are fair enough, in exceptional circumstances.

'I only go up to the attic, Mum.' Stacey pointed to the ceiling. 'I'm up there every afternoon.'

Mum stared at the ceiling in astonishment. 'You go up to the attic, Stacey dear? You sit up there in the attic, all by yourself?'

'There aren't any other children with me,' said Stacey.

'Yes, but—' Mum was bewildered. 'Yes, but—' she repeated, still staring at the ceiling '—is it any fun up there?'

Stacey rose to her feet. Visiting time in the attic was due in a couple of minutes' time. 'Fun's not the word, exactly,' she told Mum. 'But I like it up there!'

Mum went to the apartment door with Stacey.

'Oh, and I need a bit of water,' said Stacey. 'I've got the cactus up in the attic, you see. It needs watering. And while we're on the subject, the person who broke in and sneezed was me!'

Mum went into the kitchen and got Stacey a glass of water for the cactus. Before handing it over, she said, 'But it would be so nice out of doors today! Wouldn't you like to go to the zoo?'

Stacey shook her head. 'Another time, perhaps,' she said. Taking the glass of water, she went upstairs. Before going into the attic, she leaned over the banisters and waved to Mum.

She thought she had now calmed Mum's fears and restored the 'basis of trust', but unfortunately she was quite wrong. Stacey's mum was even more worried than before her serious talk with her daughter. Previously she had simply suspected that Stacey had a new friend and was spending the afternoons with him or her, and this new friend was the kind of child described as 'no sort of company for you'. She had thought this was why Stacey didn't mention her new friend, and told lies about Tina, and parties, and cacti for birthday presents. This had annoyed Mum, but she had not thought it very serious. However, a daughter who has stopped playing with other children, and quarrelled with her friend, and doesn't go to parties but spends her afternoons in the attic alone with a cactus—that did strike Mum as serious. The longer she thought about it, the more certain she felt that Stacey, her own dear Stacey, must be going through a mental crisis!

It was neither curiosity nor malice that made Stacey's mum creep up the stairs to the attic: it was sympathy! Perhaps she's sitting up there crying, thought Mum. Perhaps she'll feel better if I comfort her and take her to the zoo. She does love the lion cubs.

Mum stopped outside the attic door. She wanted to construct a sentence with which to open the conversation. Talking to unhappy and mentally disturbed children isn't easy. You have to go carefully!

As Mum stood there constructing her sentence, she heard Stacey's voice. 'Honestly, Rosa, it's the end!' Stacey was saying. 'First of all our English teacher went away for two weeks, not that we learn anything when he's around either, and then we get a test, and then he hands out Ds to almost everyone. The only reason I got an A was because I've been on holiday to England three times, and the others can't help it if they haven't been to England themselves, can they?'

Stacey's mother instantly forgot all her careful, nicely constructed sentences.

So she was lying again, she thought. She's not alone in that attic at all! There's somebody with her, somebody called Rosa!

Then Mum heard Stacey's voice again. 'And he's even beastlier when he takes gym! He keeps telling Tina to climb ropes, and he knows perfectly well she can't. And when poor Tina's hanging on the end of the rope, panting, he says, "Come along, fatty, come along!" and everyone else in our class laughs!'

Mum opened the door, just a crack. She wanted to see this Rosa. Then maybe she'd find out why Stacey utterly refused to say a word about her. Mum could see the velvet sofa through the crack. She saw Stacey sitting cross-legged on the sofa, she even saw the cactus standing in front of the sofa, she also saw her old red alarm clock— but she saw no sign of any Rosa.

Stacey was now saying, 'It's everybody laughing I mind most. I mean, I know it looks funny, fat Tina hanging there with the rope dangling between her fat legs like a tail, but they don't have to laugh at her! We all ought to stick together, don't you think?'

And then a deep, soft voice said, 'Ah, you've only been at your new school a year, you and those other children. Get to know each other a bit better and you'll stick together right enough!'

That was definitely no child's voice, Mum decided. No, it was obviously an old, old woman's voice! But where was the old, old woman? For there was no doubt about it, the voice came from the old velvet sofa!

Mum screwed up her eyes so as to see better, since it was rather dark in the attic. And then, above the far corner of the sofa, she saw Stacey's bright green knitting. Hanging in the air, busily knitting itself. And the gentle old woman's voice went on, 'How was maths, then?'

'Nothing special,' said Stacey. 'Hans got D again, but he gets D for everything. Actually, he almost always *knows* everything before the lesson, it's just that he gets all confused because he's so scared!'

'Who's he scared of then?' asked the soft voice.

Mum felt gooseflesh, cold as ice, slowly creeping up from her heels, over her legs and her hips, and rising to her neck.

'His parents get cross,' said Stacey.

Mum saw the bright green knitting suddenly drift towards Stacey. It stopped in front of her and moved gently back and forth. 'Want me to cast off the armholes now?' asked the soft voice.

'Yes, I think so! Three stitches at the beginning of the next two rows, two stitches on the next two, and then one stitch three times, Rosa,' said Stacey, and the piece of knitting drifted back to the far corner of the sofa.

'Dear, darling Rosa,' said Stacey, hopefully, 'couldn't you help Hans not to be quite so scared? I mean, if you—'

But the soft voice interrupted her. 'No, I couldn't! Old Rosa here's staying in this building! Flat feet old Rosa's got, ducky, and if she goes out people tread on 'em, see?'

'But suppose I brought Hans here, Rosa dear?'

The soft voice interrupted her again. 'No! We don't want folk talking! Who knows what it'd lead to? I don't know the lad, and you could be wrong about him! We can't tell how he'd act if he met a ghost, can we, now?'

Mum quietly closed the attic door. She was feeling so weak and unwell that she couldn't walk a step. She sat down at the top of the attic stairs. She sat there for over half an hour, listening to Stacey talking about school. And the teachers and pupils. And the caretaker. Stacey said that it wasn't all that easy, getting good marks. It made you feel guilty. Sometimes she didn't know something herself, but the teachers were never cross with *her*. The other children were nasty to her later, though.

Mum heard what Stacey was saying all right, but she didn't really take it in. She was waiting for the soft, deep voice all the time, and when it started talking she jumped.

When the half hour was over, Mum felt strong enough for the stairs again. She tottered down the eighteen steps. She would certainly have stumbled if she hadn't been clinging to the banisters. She was still covered with goose-flesh up to her neck, and now she was sweating too. A cold sweat. Mum went into the apartment, closed the door and stood in front of the big mirror in the hall. She looked at her pale face in the glass. She wiped the cold sweat from her forehead with one hand, smoothed down her hair with the other, and muttered, 'Poor Annemarie, poor, poor Annemarie, you've gone right out of your mind!'

(Stacey's mother's first name was Annemarie.)

11

Stacey stayed up in the attic longer than usual that day. It was the old red alarm clock's fault. The clock was over an hour slow. When Stacey heard the announcer start the six o'clock radio news down in Mrs Berger's apartment she jumped up in horror. 'I've still got my maths homework to do, Rosa!' she cried. 'And a composition to give in tomorrow too!'

'I'll dictate you the composition this evening, ducky,' Rosa promised. Rosa liked compositions. 'Exciting, they are,' she used to say.

'The subject's "An Old Umbrella Tells Its Story", though,' said Stacey. Rosa snorted. 'What a subject! Can't the old bag think of anything better, then? Ridiculous, that's what I call it!' Last week Rosa had written Stacey a composition called 'An Old Car Tells Its Story', and the week before she had written another called 'An Old Hat Tells Its Story'.

'You just tell the silly creature to think up something different for a change!' said Rosa Riedel.

Stacey laughed. 'You seem to think it's easy! Would *you* have dared try a thing like that when you were my age?' Rosa admitted that no, when she was Stacey's age she wouldn't have dared try a thing like that either.

'But I'll think of something by eight, don't you worry,' she promised. 'Reckon I'll write it about old Mr Dostal's umbrella, the one that was so like our landlord's! Only old Dostal's had a hole in it, see? And they got their umbrellas mixed up in the café, and our landlord thought old Mr Dostal did it on purpose, and he took him to court, and everyone in the building had to give evidence!'

Rosa Riedel sounded pleased. You could tell she was already writing this story in her head.

Stacey sighed. 'She'll say it's too far-fetched. She doesn't like compositions to be far-fetched.'

Rosa Riedel snorted crossly. 'But that's the way it was! It's not far-fetched, not a bit of it!'

'She'll say so, all the same!' Stacey had already had some trouble at school over Rosa Riedel's last two compositions. In 'An Old Car Tells Its Story', Rosa had dictated, '. . . and then my owner yelled, "Bloody hell, the sonofabitch won't start!"' And in the story about the old hat, Rosa had dictated, 'Once upon a time I was a lovely bit of felt, all pink and soft, but they bent me all whichways, knocked a hollow in the top of me, and stuck black felt flowers all over me, and then this fat woman with a great big mole on her chin bought me . . . '

Stacey had protested about the 'sonofabitch', and in particular about the 'bloody hell', because she knew the German teacher did not care for such expressions. She was dubious about the hat too, because the German teacher happened to have a hat very like the one Rosa was describing. The German teacher also had a very large mole, although hers was on her left cheek. However, Rosa Riedel had insisted that she was only sticking to the facts in every case. 'That's just the way it was,' she said. 'I heard the man yelling at his car, those were his very words, and goodness knows I had to look at our landlady in that hat often enough, with the mole on her chin!' If something is true, said Rosa, if something is no more than the facts, then you can write it down, can't you? You ought to have enough moral courage for that. Anyway, she added, Stacey got all As at school, right? Children who get all As can afford a bit of moral courage.

Stacey did feel that twice was enough to display her

moral courage to the German teacher, but she wasn't going to argue the point with Rosa just now. Anyway, it was Friday, when Mum and Dad went out, so she could talk it over at length with Rosa that evening.

'See you at eight, then, Rosa!' was all Stacey said.

'Yes, ducky,' murmured Rosa, and Stacey went downstairs.

Dad was home already. He was in the kitchen peeling potatoes. 'Come on, Stacey, give us a hand,' he said. 'Mum's not feeling well!'

Stacey went into the kitchen, picked up a potato and began peeling it. She asked what was the matter with Mum. A headache, or sore throat, or a stomach upset? Dad answered evasively. Well, he said, he couldn't say exactly. Mum was just feeling rather tired, but she might be better in an hour or so.

Dad had no intention of telling Stacey the truth. The truth was that on coming home, Dad had found Mum in the bedroom, lying on the bed with her eyes closed, not moving. When Dad approached the bed, she had asked, 'Bertie, are there any such things as ghosts?'

'No!' said Dad, laughing.

Upon which, Mum had raised herself slightly from the bed and whispered, 'In that case, I'm crazy! I'm awfully sorry, Bertie, but I really can't help it!' And then she dropped back on the bed and lay there not moving again.

Dad sat on the edge of the bed patting Mum. After a bit of this, Mum had sobbed that her nerves must be in a frightful state, she was right off her head, she was stark staring mad, and at this precise moment she did not, *not* want to see another living soul.

Dad left the bedroom, went into the kitchen and started to peel potatoes. So there he still was, peeling potatoes, making out to Stacey that Mum was just 'rather tired'.

'You mean you two aren't going out this evening?' asked Stacey anxiously. Dad just shrugged his shoulders. Stacey wanted to go into the bedroom to take a look at her poor tired mother, but Dad was against this. 'We'll make some chips,' he said, 'and cook a steak, and have something to eat, and then I'll take a look at Mum myself.'

'But if she's hungry—'said Stacey.

'She's tired,' said Dad.

'Tired people can be hungry too!'

'No!' said Dad. 'She's asleep.'

Stacey cut the potatoes into chips, and heated the fat in the chip pan, thinking: Dad's in a very strange mood today. She kept glancing anxiously at the kitchen clock. It was getting later and later. She had to know if her parents were going out or staying in. Rosa was used to just ringing the doorbell on evenings her parents were out. She much preferred that to getting into the apartment from the passage and through the open window of the boxroom.

The chips were fried, the steaks were cooked, it was already seven-thirty. Stacey and Dad sat down at the table.

'Look, Dad,' said Stacey, 'you really must go and ask Mum if she still wants to go to the theatre, or it'll be too late.'

Dad hesitated. 'Well, I don't know—' he said.

'If you don't ask her, I will!' said Stacey.

'Eat your supper!' said Dad.

And then Mum came in. She walked as if she had not quite recovered from a long and serious illness. Her hair was untidy, there wasn't a trace of make-up left on her face, and she was clinging to the walls to support herself as she went along.

Stacey immediately saw that her poor tired mother would not be going out again today.

Mum tottered into the kitchen and dropped into one of

the kitchen chairs.

'Feeling better, darling?' asked Dad, concerned.

'Thanks, yes, I'm better,' said Mum, quietly, but it did not sound very convincing.

'Shall I cook you a steak?' asked Dad.

'A steak?' murmured Mum. 'A steak?' You might have thought she had never heard the word before in her life, although steak was her favourite food.

'Or would you like to go back to bed?' Dad did not think that such a confused, distraught mother was a fit sight for his daughter.

'No, I'll stay here with you two,' murmured Mum. 'I don't want to be alone. I'm frightened.'

Dad tried to act as if he had not heard this. He asked Stacey about school, about Tina, about Tommy and Michael. Stacey told him how she was the only one to get A in English. That came easily, since it was the third time she had told the story today. As she was telling it she searched her mind feverishly for some excuse to go up to the attic. 'Why don't I take Mrs Berger a slice of apple strudel?' would have been a possibility, but unfortunately there was no apple strudel in the apartment. What else could she take Mrs Berger? A bottle of beer? A tin-opener? A can of pineapple rings? The supermarket's special offers leaflet? A newspaper? The television programmes! That sounded likely! Mrs Berger often did lose her guide to the television programmes. and then she came over to borrow one. Stacey ended the tale of how she got A for English, '. . . and after all, the others can't help not having been to England three times, can they?' and then she got up, carried the pile of dirty dishes to the sink, and said, 'Oh, I almost forgot! Mrs Berger asked me to take the telly programmes over! I said I would.'

'There's a copy under the sofa,' said Dad.

Stacey went into the living room, knelt down by the sofa, groped under it for the television programmes and fished the copy out. At that moment the front doorbell rang. Short, short, long, long! That was Rosa Riedel!

Stacey had no chance to reach the front door first. Dad was closer. Three strides took him to the door. He opened it, and looked out into the empty passage in surprise.

'Hello—anyone there?' he called. 'What's the idea?' He stepped out into the passage, looked down the stairs, listened, but there were no footsteps to be heard. He came back into the apartment, closed the door and said, shaking his head, 'Well, I don't know! The bell ringing, and not a soul in sight!'

Mum jumped up from the kitchen chair. Her eyes were round with fright, and she was trembling all over.

'Let's go to the theatre, Bertie!' she cried.

'It's too late, darling!'

'Well, we can go in at the beginning of the second act!'

'By the time you've changed and done your hair,' said Dad, 'the second act will be over too.'

'Then we'll go to the café, or a bar, or out for a walk, or anywhere you like!' Mum's voice was shrill. 'I'm not staying in a place where the bell rings and there's nobody at the door! My nerves won't stand it!'

'Listen, Annemarie,' said Dad, 'the bell must have gone wrong. A loose connection or something like that.'

'Loose connection nothing!' screeched Mum. 'That was no loose connection! That was never any loose connection! Somebody rang the bell!'

'Oh yes!' said Dad. 'And *who* rang the bell, then?'

For a moment it looked as if Mum was going to tell him, but then she murmured, 'Sorry, Bertie. Yes, of course it was some kind of loose connection!'

Stacey was standing in the open doorway. She could feel

Rosa Riedel beside her, all warm and soft like a huge balloon. Stacey groped for Rosa's hand, found it and held it tight. She heard Rosa Riedel saying quietly, but quite distinctly, 'My word, what a fuss the woman does make!'

Dad heard the quiet voice too. However, he didn't let it baffle him for more than a moment before deciding that he had been listening to his own thoughts. At the same time he decided to take Mum to the café, for coffee and a cream slice. He must take her mind off her troubles or she'd go quite crazy. And perhaps in the café, when Stacey wasn't with them, she would tell him what got her into such a state.

Dad fetched Mum's jacket from the hall and held it out to her. 'Come along, darling, let's go to the café then!'

Mum had one arm in her jacket sleeve when she suddenly said, 'I can't leave Stacey on her own!'

'But we go out every Friday, darling!' said Dad. 'Stacey's not a bit scared now!'

'It's a terrible thing to do,' muttered Mum, but she let Dad get her into her jacket. She just stood there like an old-fashioned doll with jointed limbs, waiting for him to button it up, and pull the sleeves straight, and then propel her through the doorway.

At the door Dad heard his own thoughts again. They were saying in a soft, deep and slightly anxious tone, 'What's she carrying on like that for, then?' And then he heard Stacey say, 'Oh, do be quiet!' Since Dad did not suppose Stacey could hear his thoughts as well, he told himself: good heavens, now I'm saying things out loud when I only meant to think them. No wonder, though! She'll drive me out of my own mind yet!

Stacey and Rosa waited until the sound of Dad and Mum's footsteps had died away.

'Your mum's overdoing it,' said Rosa. 'No call to carry on like that just because the doorbell rings!'

'She was in a peculiar mood before,' said Stacey.

Rosa sighed, deeply. 'Ah,' she said. 'Then she's found us out, ducky, that's what it is.'

'What are we going to do?' Stacey put two fingers in her mouth and bit the nails.

'Stop biting your nails, for a start!' Rosa told her. 'Makes me nervous, nail-biting does!'

Obediently, Stacey took her fingers out of her mouth and followed Rosa into her own room. 'Now you just do your sums,' Rosa told her, 'and I'll sketch out that composition, and when you've done your sums I'll dictate it, then we'll discuss what to do about your mum, right?'

Stacey agreed. She sat down at her desk and worked out how many builders it would take to build a wall in eight hours if it took nine builders 14 hours 23 minutes to build the same wall.

Opposite Stacey, on the other side of the desk, there was a large, lined notepad, and a green pencil was writing spiky letters on this pad.

'Only two pages, though,' said Stacey to the green pencil. 'Please don't get carried away again! I don't want to write a long composition!'

Yet again, of course, Rosa failed to limit herself to two pages. Stacey had to take down eight closely written pages of dictation before the old umbrella—the one with the hole in it—finally ended its exciting career down in the cellar with the solid fuel briquettes and the jam jars.

Then Rosa sat in the rocking chair, rocked herself, and said, 'Well, ducky, I've been thinking. Reckon I'd better stay down here tonight, just in case your mum throws another fit of hysterics!'

'Don't say hysterics!' said Stacey. 'It sounds horrible. Mum's frightened, that's all. Grown-ups find it hard to take a ghost, you said so yourself. But you wouldn't understand about being frightened, of course.'

'Oh, wouldn't I just!' said Rosa. 'I get frightened too, ducky. Very frightened.'

'Well, maybe you used to. When you were still alive,' said Stacey. 'But not now!'

'You bet I used to!' said Rosa. 'Those were frightening times! But I do still get frightened, believe you me!'

This was no lie. Rosa Riedel suffered from a phobia. Ever since she was buried under the rubble of Mrs Wokurka's building, Rosa had been afraid of being shut up in small spaces: afraid of chimneys, cupboards, narrow passages, tiny rooms. She never went into lavatories or cellars if she could help it. And if she had to get through the boxroom window to visit Stacey, she trembled all over.

She had also had a nasty experience with a cupboard a few months ago. She had crept into Miss Dostal's flat to watch television. But she didn't like the programme, and so in order to annoy Miss Dostal, she had opened the big wardrobe out in the hall and muddled up Miss Dostal's underclothes. Miss Dostal was very neat and tidy. Nothing bothered her more than an untidy wardrobe. And she got really upset if she couldn't think why her bras and pants and nighties were in such a mess again. 'May goodness me!' she would wail. 'And Ay taidied thet wardrobe only yesterdie!'

As Rosa stood in front of the open wardrobe during the boring TV programme, mixing up Miss Dostal's bras and winter socks, and her vests and her blouses, and putting her pants on top of her handkerchiefs, Miss Dostal herself came into the hall and saw the open wardrobe door.

'Bless may soul if thet door doesn't open of its own accord!' she said, closing it. As she closed it, she felt strong resistance. 'Sticks, too! Ay must get the hinges seen to.'

Miss Dostal pushed the door with all her might. Miss

Dostal was quite a strong woman. She did it. The door shut, and Rosa was stuck inside the wardrobe.

There was plenty of room inside the wardrobe. Rosa could have made herself comfortable there. She could have settled down for a nap on three piles of angora vests and waited for Miss Dostal to open the wardrobe again, which she would be bound to do, at the latest, before she went to bed when she came to fetch a hanky for the night. But Rosa was overtaken by panic terror. She hammered on the door with both hands, moaning. And Miss Dostal, standing outside the cupboard, cried, 'Bless may soul! The wood's splitting! May wardrobe is falling to bits!' And as the wardrobe really was in a shaky state, and Rosa was hammering very hard against the door, and moreover the catch of the door was rather old and not up to much, the wardrobe finally opened and Rosa escaped.

'You were never as scared in all your life as I was then, ducky,' Rosa told Stacey.

Stacey was going to say that once—in the days before she made friends with Rosa—she'd been scared to death of dogs, empty apartments and attics, but then she heard footsteps in the hall. Mum and Dad were back. Next moment, there was Dad in the doorway of her room. He looked worn out.

'Is Mum better now?' asked Stacey.

Dad looked worried. 'I'm taking her to a doctor tomorrow,' he said quietly. 'Her nerves are in a poor way, you see: it's not serious, though, these things happen, they can cure it all right these days, you must . . . .' Here Dad stopped talking. He stared at Stacey's rocking chair. The rocking chair was rocking. Rocking quite hard. It couldn't be a draught. And nobody could have given it a push either.

'Stacey?' said Dad, raising his hand and pointing at the rocking chair. 'Stacey, how do you do that?'

'I'm not doing anything,' said Stacey, looking guilelessly at Dad. And suddenly the rocking chair stopped rocking. 'What are you talking about?' asked Stacey.

'The rocking chair,' faltered Dad, 'the rocking chair . . . .'

'What about it?' asked Stacey.

'Oh, nothing,' said Dad, and he added, 'Good night, Stacey, off you go to bed, it's getting late,' and went out of the room. Stacey heard him out in the hall, muttering to himself, 'There's a rational explanation for everything, there's a rational explanation for everything, if only you can find it!'

12

Stacey slept badly that night. She woke up several times. It was not just Mum's loud, shrill voice and Dad's quiet, worried voice carrying as far as her room: Rosa Riedel, in the rocking chair, was snoring dreadfully. Sometimes it was like a saw going through thick planks, sometimes it was like an old locomotive making its final run, and sometimes Rosa just gurgled like a bath with the plughole partly stopped up.

If Stacey had not known for certain that it was her guardian ghost sawing and snorting and gurgling away, she would surely have been terrified. As she did know, she was not frightened, and whenever the snoring woke her she picked up the glass paperweight from her bedside table and knocked it against the edge of the bed a few times. Then Rosa quietened down for a while.

Towards morning, Rosa stopped snoring altogether, and as Stacey's parents had stopped talking too she was able to sleep soundly. Indeed, she slept so soundly that she didn't wake up until seven instead of six-thirty, and then it was only because of the cars hooting down in the street outside her window. (They were trying to hoot a truck parked in the right-hand lane out of their way.)

'Are you still asleep, Rosa?' Stacey asked the rocking chair as she got out of bed. There was no answer. Going over to the rocking chair, she put out her hand and felt nothing but cold, thin air.

Stacey skimped on cleaning her teeth and washing her neck and ears, did her hair in record time, flung on the clothes she had taken off last night, and was amazed to find that she was now ready five minutes earlier than usual.

Adding the time usually spent on her morning visit to the attic, she still had fifteen minutes before she need start for school.

There was no one in the kitchen but Dad. He was crouching on the floor, cursing and wiping it with a cloth. He had poured too much water into the coffee filter, and coffee was dripping out of the glass jug, over the dresser and on to the floor.

Stacey clambered over Dad, took the filter out of the glass jug and threw it away. 'Or you'll just be wiping it up for ever,' she told him. Dad muttered that he was no good in the mornings. He could make the best coffee in the world at night, but in the morning he wasn't even in a fit state to boil water.

Stacey avoided asking any questions about Mum. She looked around for some form of nourishment suitable for breakfast. (Since making friends with Rosa, she found she was enormously hungry every morning.) But there wasn't a slice of fresh bread to be found anywhere, no milk either, and the tea canister contained nothing but a few tealeaves the size of baby ants.

Stacey got a bottle of Coca-Cola out of the fridge. She poured it into a glass, sat down at the kitchen table and drank ice-cold Coke. Dad came over to the table with the full jug of coffee. Since it was filled to the brim, and Dad did not want to spill any more coffee, he kept his eyes firmly on the jug as he carried it. Thus he failed to see the kitchen bin standing in the middle of the kitchen. (Stacey had put it there because she was going to empty it. Emptying the rubbish and the wastepaper basket were part of her household chores.) Dad stumbled over the bin. It fell over, emptying large quantities of disgusting rubbish out on the kitchen floor. Dad dropped the jug of coffee in alarm. Hot coffee spilled partly on the floor, partly on the rubbish, and partly on the legs of Dad's pale grey trousers.

Dad looked so funny standing there in the middle of all the rubbish that Stacey couldn't help laughing. This infuriated Dad, who was not an even-tempered person.

'Stop laughing in that stupid way and help me!' shouted Dad. 'First you put the rubbish where I'll fall over it, then you sit there laughing!'

However, Stacey simply could not stop laughing, which infuriated Dad even more. He made for Stacey. No one could tell, afterwards, whether he was going to slap her or just shout at her from closer to.

Dad's right foot trod on a soft piece of mouldy cheese. His left foot trod on a bit of pancake. The pancake and the cheese stuck to the soles of his shoes, making them extremely slippery. Dad slipped. He did not actually fall over, because he managed to catch hold of the side of the table with one hand, but he had to put a knee on the ground. And as the table itself began to wobble, Stacey's glass of Coke fell over, and the Coke was spilt on Dad's jacket. Dad roared with fury and disgust as if a dozen wasps had stung him. He flung his arms about as if another dozen wasps were threatening to attack. He flapped at the eggshells, potato peelings, grains of rice and dust sticking to his suit. 'It's all your fault!' he yelled at Stacey. 'Just look at this! And my other suit's at the cleaners! And I have to go to the official opening of that ruddy school! I can't go in a check sports jacket, can I? All because of you!'

Stacey tried wiping Dad clean with large pieces torn off the roll of kitchen paper. It was a waste of effort, but Stacey still went on wiping. Perhaps he'll calm down a bit, she thought. Wiping's much the same as stroking.

Dad did not calm down at all. 'Stop that!' he yelled. 'It's no earthly use trying to clean that lot off! Stop that stupid wiping!'

Stacey dropped the kitchen paper. Dad took a deep breath in order to go on yelling at her. For the fraction of a second, all was perfectly still in the kitchen, and then a deep, soft voice said, 'Now you just go easy on that shouting, young man! It's not Stacey's fault you can't see a kitchen bin as big as an elephant! And don't you gawp in that silly way either, young man! I'm Rosa Riedel. Been invisible since I died, I'm sorry to say. Now then, you go and take that suit off, and Stacey, you can bring me a dustpan and brush!'

Stacey hurried off to the broom cupboard for the dustpan and brush and put them down by the heap of rubbish on the kitchen floor. Then she got a cloth and wiped the spilt Coke off the table.

Dad stood there, perfectly still, straight as a ramrod and frozen rigid, as if struck by a bolt of icy lightning. Down at his feet, the brush busily piled rubbish into the dustpan. The dustpan floated over to the bin, emptied itself, returned to the brush and let the brush fill it again.

'Well, get a move on, young man,' said the deep voice, no longer sounding very soft. 'Take that suit off, I said! Your ears stopped up, are they?'

The rubbish was back in the bin now. So were the bits of broken glass. The cupboard door under the sink opened, the floorcloth floated out and up to the tap, water began to flow from the tap, the wet floorcloth wrung itself into a thick sausage shape. Dad still stood there, thunderstruck.

Stacey was standing by the kitchen window, two fingers in her mouth, biting her nails. She was afraid that Dad, like Mum, might assume he was crazy and retire to bed.

The wet cloth was now on the floor, moving quickly back and forth. 'Take those shoes of yours off at least, do!' said the deep voice. 'That cheese and the bit of pancake are still sticking to them. Take another step and they'll get everywhere again! Need a valet, do you, young man?'

At last Dad moved. He stepped out of his shoes, and no sooner was he out of them than they floated over to the sink, soles upward. A knife flew towards them, scraped the pancake and cheese off, the plastic sponge hopped over to wipe the soles, and the deep voice remarked, 'There we are, then!'

Dad took off his jacket, moving slowly, like a sleepwalker: then, even more slowly, he undid the buckle of his belt and pulled the belt out of its loops.

'I thought you were in a hurry,' snapped Rosa Riedel. 'Look sharp, now! Or maybe you're shy of me, is that it? Don't let it worry you! I've been around for a hundred and five years. Plenty of gentlemen I've seen, in all sorts of different underpants!'

Dad unzipped his trousers and took them off. Stacey got the spot cleaner aerosol out of the kitchen cupboard, but Rosa didn't want it. She said she didn't think much of such new-fangled stuff. She scrubbed the trousers with lukewarm water. 'Get at a mark at once and it'll soon go,' she muttered. 'It's just those ads make you think you need a different sort of cleaner for every little thing!' Rosa scrubbed at Dad's jacket too, using water and a little soap, and then she sent Stacey to find the iron and ironing board.

Dad sat down in a chair, the picture of what is thought of as 'a broken man'. Stacey was biting her fingernails, determined not to interfere. Rosa could cope with this on her own! She was sure to be better at it! (Pressing suits as well as explaining ghosts to Dad.)

When the suit was pressed, Rosa said, 'Now, it just needs a little time to dry, and while it's drying I'll make breakfast!'

'There isn't anything for breakfast, Rosa,' said Stacey.

'Nonsense!' The lower drawers of the dresser swung open. 'Seeing as you two don't trouble your heads with housekeeping, you don't know anything about it!'

A carton of long-life milk and a packet of crispbread made their way out of the dresser, followed by the cocoa. The gas flared up, the milk pan jumped on the flame, and then the long-life milk floated through the air, stopped in front of Dad's nose, and the deep voice said, 'Now then, young man, open me this carton! I never used any milk like *this* before!' Dad reached for the scissors hanging on a hook on the wall by the table, but as Rosa was between him and the hook he was unable to get them. His hand met the soft warmth of Rosa.

'Don't look so scared, it's only me,' said the deep voice. 'There, I've moved now. Never could stand being tickled!' And Dad could reach the scissors. He cut off a corner of the carton and hesitantly held it up.

'I'm not that tall!' said the deep voice. Dad lowered the carton and Rosa took it. 'Thanks!' she said.

Five minutes later, Dad and Stacey were eating crispbread with butter, jam and ham, and drinking cocoa, and Rosa Riedel was sitting on the empty chair between them. 'You'll have to excuse me for snapping at you to start with, young man,' she told Dad. 'It's my experience that shock therapy's the only way a person can take ghosts. You just got to *be* there all of a sudden, I mean, without a lot of explanation first. The longer the likes of us spend preparing people, the more carefully we go about it, the sillier folk act!' And she added kindly, 'I'll give you your due, young man, you stood up to it pretty well. One time when I couldn't avoid meeting old Franz, he started right in there praying. And he's not been to church since 'thirty-eight! And Mrs Berger locked herself in the toilet when I was watching television round at her place, a very funny film it was, and I couldn't help laughing a couple of times! Yes, young man, you're almost as sensible as your daughter!'

Dad seemed pleased by this praise, and yet Stacey thought he somehow still had the look of a broken man. So she said, 'You know, Dad, I really am very glad I've got Rosa. Actually we always did have her, only we didn't know it.'

Dad sighed.

'You can leave off sighing, young man,' said Rosa Riedel. 'You just be glad you had somebody to clean that suit up! And wash the floor. Clumsy as you are, you'd still be standing around in all the mess!'

'Yes,' said Dad, sighing again, 'yes, of course, only the thing is, you see, it upsets my entire view of life.'

'Nonsense!' said Rosa briskly. 'I never upset anybody's view of life, not me! The rich stay rich and the poor stay poor, don't they, even if they know there's a ghost around the place? And you won't be changing your notions of what's good and bad just because you've had to take notice of me, will you? Or were you thinking of voting a different way at the next election, because you've found out anything's possible? Now that *would* be silly! You'll vote the way you ought to vote, of course!'

'How do you know what way I vote?' asked Dad, bewildered.

Rosa laughed. 'Been in this building longer than you, haven't I? I've been getting into the apartment through the boxroom window ever since you moved in! Well, stands to reason I know all about you! Couldn't be helped, could it?'

Suddenly there were footsteps out in the hall. Next moment Mum came into the kitchen. Pale and heavy-eyed and haggard. 'Haven't you two left yet?' she asked. 'It's eight-thirty!'

Mum went to sit on the empty kitchen chair.

'Stop!' Dad jumped up. 'Don't! Rosa Riedel's sitting in that one!' Mum stared at the empty chair. Dad put an arm round her shoulders.

'Ah, well,' said Rosa, sighing. 'Looks to me like I'll have to materialize again! Now watch carefully, young woman. I can't keep it up long, this materializing lark!'

Mum watched carefully. So did Dad and Stacey. This time Rosa managed to materialize much better than before. You could even see that her fingers were dirty from washing the floor, and she had a large varicose vein on her right leg.

'Oh, don't go yet! Do stay!' Stacey begged, as Rosa turned paler and more transparent.

'Heaven forbid!' panted Rosa, and then she was gone. 'Talk about an effort! Makes you come out in a sweat, and your head's left ringing!' She moaned softly. 'Yes, I've got a headache again, sure enough! I'm going to bed. See you later!'

The empty chair was pushed back to the wall, something soft and warm made its way past Mum and Dad, and then the front door of the apartment opened and closed again.

'Have we all three gone out of our minds now?' asked Mum, but her voice was reasonably steady, and she was not shaking at all.

'I honestly can't see why you have to make such a fuss!' said Stacey. 'There *are* such things as ghosts. So what? She's proved it, hasn't she?' And then Stacey told them everything she knew about the life and death of Rosa Riedel, the Nazi stormtroopers, the jars of jam and the bacon, and how Rosa pinched the Hitler Youth boys, and scared the landlady, and was buried in the rubble and had a phobia afterwards, so that now she didn't dare to leave the building.

'Well,' said Mum, 'at least one thing's obvious, that's the first right-thinking ghost I ever heard of!'

'I wish I didn't have to go,' said Dad, 'but I really must

leave for the opening of that school now! I'll be very late as it is!' He put his trousers and jacket on and slipped his belt through its loops. Then he kissed Mum. 'Are you still frightened, darling? Would you like Stacey to stay with you?'

Mum said she was hardly frightened at all now. She could cope with what little fright she had left.

'Come on, then, Stacey,' said Dad. 'I'll drive you to school.'

Stacey fetched her satchel and ran downstairs after Dad. She heard him muttering, 'If I were to tell this to anyone else at the Ministry . . . .'

'I wouldn't, Dad,' said Stacey.

'You bet I won't!' said Dad. 'I don't want to end up out of my job or in a mental home!'

At the front door of the building, Stacey told Dad, 'You'll like Rosa Riedel, Dad, really you will!'

In the car, Stacey told Dad, 'Rosa Riedel is a lovely person, Dad! Really useful too!'

As she got out of the car at school, Stacey told Dad, 'You'll soon wonder how you ever managed without Rosa Riedel.'

And each time Dad replied, 'I only hope you're right!'

13

What with all the excitement of that morning, of course Stacey had forgotten to ask Mum or Dad for an excuse note. She hadn't even thought of any good reason for being late. Even once she was in school and going along the corridor to her classroom, she thought of nothing but Rosa Riedel, and she went with a hop, skip and a jump, because Mum was not 'crazy' any longer, and Dad believed in Rosa, and there was a basis of trust in their family again. Stacey felt happy.

And then she opened the classroom door and saw a crowd of children sitting perfectly still, staring at her, and up at the front by the board was the German teacher, who had not been at all nice to Stacey since that composition about the old hat which was so like her own.

'Late, but I suppose it's something you're here at all!' remarked the German teacher, in the direction of the door.

'Please, I—I mean it was—well, I couldn't. . . .'

The German teacher shook her head crossly. 'You mean what? You couldn't what? Can't you put a sentence together any more?'

Some of the class laughed. Tina didn't.

'Now, may I hear just why you are late, Stacey? Take your time! Perhaps you've brought an excuse note?' And the German teacher put out her hand for the note.

'I'm sorry, I haven't got one,' said Stacey. 'I'll bring it tomorrow.'

'Then as your class mistress, may I be allowed to know why you don't get to school till nine-thirty?' Some of the children laughed again. Stacey felt miserable. All the happiness of a moment ago had melted away. 'Well, what is it, Stacey? Come along, speak up! You're not usually at a loss for words!'

Fancy being so horrible because of an old hat! Fancy taking such offence at a 'bloody hell'! The German teacher had always been nice to her before Rosa's first composition. Very nice, in fact!

'I see,' said the German teacher. 'You would rather not tell us. Very well. Kindly go to your desk and don't disturb the lesson any more.'

Stacey went to her desk and sat down, expecting Tina's triumphant look. Tina tore a page out of her rough book and scribbled, 'Take it easy! She's really mad!' Tina pushed the note over to Stacey, who gratefully accepted this peace offering with a nod. Then she took her pen, her exercise book and her textbook out of her satchel. She thought: I just hope Miss Spitz (this was the German teacher's name) doesn't ask to hear my composition now, or she'll flip her lid! (For there were a great many improper words in Rosa Riedel's latest effort.) However, no sooner had Stacey arranged her school things neatly on the desk than the bell went for break. She heaved a sigh of relief.

'I have not yet ended the lesson, you know!' said the German teacher. A few children had started chattering away to each other. She banged her desk with her textbook. 'The lesson ends when I say so, not at the bell!' The class fell silent again. 'Very well,' said the teacher. 'The lesson is over now.' She strode towards the door, and Stacey heaved a second sigh of relief, but at the door the German teacher turned again and said, 'I should like another word with you, Stacey!'

Stacey followed her out into the corridor. 'I am very disappointed in you, Stacey!' said the German teacher. 'I seem to have been wrong about you!' And she went on to say that when their class started at this school, she had thought Stacey was a bright, friendly, well-mannered child. So she had given her an A in her term report, and said nice things to her mother on Speech Day. Over the last month, however, she said Stacey had changed completely! She hardly took any part in lessons, she looked out of the window in a bored way, and when she was asked a question she often didn't even know what it had been. She herself, said Miss Spitz, was not the only one to have noticed: some of the other teachers had commented on it too! However, one might let that pass! Schoolchildren were often ignorant and found it hard to concentrate. What could not be allowed to pass, however, was Stacey's written composition work, which really was scraping the bottom of the barrel! It was just too much.

'There's nothing for it, Stacey,' said the German teacher, ominously. 'I shall be obliged to have a word with your father about these compositions!' Obviously there must be a great many children to whom the idea of a teacher's having a word with their father was terrifying. It was not terrifying to Stacey, far from it. Let Dad deal with it! Dad would be better than Stacey at telling the German teacher why it was all right to put 'bloody hell' in a composition. He had already explained to Mum. (Mum had looked through the old car composition for spelling mistakes, and found none, but said the expressions 'bloody hell' and 'sonofabitch' were a bit too vulgar to be used in a school composition.)

So Stacey nodded at the German teacher, said she was sure that her father would be coming to Parents' Evening next Monday, and thought that was the end of the conversation. But then the German teacher asked if Stacey's Dad was '*the* Dr Sommer, of the Ministry of Education' and when Stacey nodded she started saying what a shame it was for a child to grieve such a 'nice, kind, good father', and for the daughter of Dr Sommer of the Ministry, of all people, to produce such 'absolutely impossible work'.

If Stacey had written the compositions herself, she would have kept her mouth shut, but this was a matter of defending Rosa. ('And a person that won't stand up for her friends is no good, ducky,' Rosa had told her quite recently.)

So Stacey cleared her throat, and said, 'My father read both compositions, and he thought they were good!' (In point of fact, Dad had laughed a great deal at the compositions and said he thought they were marvellous.) The German teacher made a face as if she were sucking a sour lemon, and then she turned and marched off to the staffroom.

Some of the children from Stacey's class, including Michael and Hans, were standing in the classroom door. They had heard the whole thing, and when the German teacher disappeared into the staffroom they came over to Stacey and congratulated her on her courage. 'You were terrific!' said Michael. 'I'd never have dared! She was just about bursting with rage!'

But Hans did not congratulate Stacey. 'Don't you really mind her wanting to speak to your father?' he asked

'Oh, go on! My dad will just laugh!' said Stacey, but then, knowing that Hans had a father who got cross with him, and not wishing to boast of her own excellent father, she added, 'He's got a lot of other faults, though! He nearly hit me this morning just for leaving the bin in the middle of the kitchen.'

This pleased Hans. His father had never hit him for leaving a bin in the wrong place. (Hans was not pleased because he wanted Stacey to be hit, but because he was now able to persuade himself that all fathers are horrible one way or another, and all children have to suffer from them.

Such things sometimes help you bear your own troubles.)

Stacey went back into the classroom with the others. Herbert was sitting at her desk. Tina was testing him on his English vocabulary. Stacey sat down on the desk top and listened.

'I just hope the English teacher's off sick again today,' said Herbert, anxiously. 'If he isn't, I bet he tests me, and I don't know it!'

'Oh, come on!' Tina comforted him. 'You got more than half of them right!'

'But I'll forget that half again when it's my turn!'

'You don't have to be tested today,' said Stacey. 'I asked my dad. He knows about these things. A teacher has to give at least two hours' advance warning of a test. And the English teacher hasn't, so he can't give a test. And if he does, then he can't count your mark for the end of term report!'

'He does test us, though,' said Tina. 'Always.'

'Only because no one's told him he can't,' Stacey explained.

'If I tell him he can't test me today, he'll shout at me and give me an E straight off,' said Herbert.

'Send your parents to see him,' Stacey advised.

Herbert shook his head. 'They won't do it. They say I'm old enough to look after myself.'

Lost in thought, Tina picked her nose, then removed her finger from her nostril, looked at it, and said, 'The class spokesman ought to talk to him. What's he supposed to be for? Not just collecting money!'

'Tommy!' called Stacey. 'Come over here, would you, Tommy?'

Tommy, who was the class spokesman, looked Stacey's way and was just coming over when the English teacher marched into the classroom. Everyone stood to attention.

The English teacher liked you to stand to attention. If you stood to attention particularly well, he would give you an easier time.

'Sit down!' said the English teacher, getting out his little notebook and leafing through it. 'Well, we've a lot to catch up with,' he murmured, 'since unfortunately I was away last week. We must make an extra effort now!' He did a bit more leafing and then called, 'Steiner.' Steiner was Gerald, not Herbert.

Gerald stood to attention.

'Your vocabulary book, please!' said the English teacher.

Gerald took his vocabulary book up to the English teacher, went back to his desk and stood to attention again.

Stacey took a scrap of paper out of her satchel and wrote, 'Tell him he has to give advance notice of tests!' She folded the note, wrote 'Tommy' on it, and threw it over to him.

The English teacher, looking through Gerald's vocabulary book, did not notice. He was marking the book with red felt pen, looking cross and muttering, 'You can't even copy things down correctly in this class! What's the matter with your brains?'

Tommy unfolded the note, read Stacey's demand and looked horrified. Turning to glance at her, he shook his head. Stacey tried to make him change his mind by means of nods and gestures, but Tommy looked away as if that were that. So Stacey wrote another, similar note and threw it over to Gabrielle. Gabrielle was Tommy's deputy. She read the note, nodded, but then pointed to Tommy, meaning: It's up to him, I'm only his deputy!

Nods and gestures were no more use. Stacey leaned forward and whispered to Michael, 'Tell Gabrielle he won't!'

Michael turned round. 'Who won't what?'

The English teacher looked briefly up from Gerald's vocabulary book. 'Quiet, please!' he said.

'Tell her, Michael!' Stacey whispered again.

'Be quiet, please, Stacey,' said the English teacher. He was very fond of Stacey, who had a good English accent and got As for her homework: Rosa Riedel had not written any English compositions for her.

'Go on!' Stacey urged Michael.

Michael whispered, 'When he's not looking.'

'Stacey, that will be quite enough,' said the English teacher. 'I take it that you are bored by the testing of the less able pupils, but you might at least show enough public spirit to sit through the process in silence!'

Stacey glanced at Tommy, who was bending over his exercise book. Stacey glanced at Gabrielle, who was still shaking her head and pointing surreptitiously at Tommy.

What was it Rosa Riedel said? 'You can't always wait for other people to get a thing done!' she used to say. 'A lot of the trouble in the world comes of folk standing by, watching, keeping quiet, waiting for other folk to take action!'

Stacey put her two fingers in her mouth and bit the nails. The English teacher shut Gerald Steiner's vocabulary book and said the mistakes he'd made in copying were enough to earn him an E as it was, but he would make allowances! He was prepared to test Gerald all the same. Perhaps Gerald would come up to the board so that nobody could whisper to him, which was not allowed.

Gerald was already on his way to the board when Stacey took her fingers out of her mouth, plucked up all her courage, rose to her feet and said, 'Please, sir, you have to give advance notice of tests!' The English teacher looked at Stacey in surprise. Gerald stationed himself by the board and waited.

'What did you say, Stacey?' asked the English teacher.

'You can't test Gerald, because you didn't say you were going to.'

The English teacher smiled. 'Ah, Miss Stacey on the barricades, eh?'

'It says in the Education Act—' Stacey began, and then hesitated, because she was not quite sure what it did say in the Education Act.

'Yes, what does it say?' asked the English teacher, still smiling.

'My father said—'

'Oh, the Education Act says your father said something?' The English teacher seemed much amused.

'No!' said Stacey. 'My father says the Education Act says teachers can't test pupils.'

'Indeed? So pupils may no longer be tested, is that it?'

'No, I mean we can still be tested, but—'

The English teacher was not letting Stacey finish. 'So I may test you after all? Well, I'm glad you'll allow that!'

Stacey was near tears. Tears of rage. It was herself she was angry with. Why hadn't she had a look at the Education Act at home? It was on Dad's desk! If she had read the paragraph about oral examination and learned it off by heart, she wouldn't be making such a fool of herself now, and the English teacher wouldn't be standing there grinning, so sure of victory, teasing her.

'Sit down and keep quiet, Stacey,' said the English teacher. 'We missed three lessons last week, and I haven't got time to argue with you.' He didn't even look angry: he was still grinning. The whole thing seemed to strike him as funny.

Stacey stayed on her feet. She was not giving in so easily. Someone who had Rosa Riedel for a guardian ghost ought to show a bit of courage.

'I meant—' Stacey began again, but the English teacher

simply turned his back on her, looked at Gerald, and started testing him on his English vocabulary.

At this Stacey felt such seething rage sweep over her that she picked up the textbook still lying on her desk and flung it on the floor. 'You're horrible!' she shouted, and ran out of the classroom, slamming the door behind her. She stumbled down the corridor to the stairs. The staffroom door was beside the stairs, and just as Stacey reached them, it opened and out came Mr Berger the history teacher. He was wearing his coat and had his briefcase under his arm. He was going home.

'Hello,' he said, 'what's the matter? Feeling ill? You look very pale!'

Stacey shook her head.

'Where are you going then, in the middle of lessons?'

Stacey had no idea where she was going. She just knew she didn't want to go back to the classroom, and she told Mr Berger so. 'He laughed at me! He doesn't take me seriously! And I'm right and he's wrong, and nobody would help me!' It took the history teacher some time to understand the ins and outs of the story, which was all Stacey's fault: not even the cleverest of people could have made much of her confused sobs. When he had finally grasped it, he advised Stacey to go straight back to the classroom. 'You can say you weren't feeling well, but you're better now,' he told her. 'And don't say anything else at all unless it's to do with the lesson.'

Stacey shook her head stubbornly. 'People have to fight for their rights!' she sobbed.

'My dear girl,' said the history teacher, 'as far as I can see you're not fighting, you're crying!' Then he explained, 'In this case, the way to fight for your rights is persuading the rest of the class to tell the spokesman to put your point in the proper way. If he won't, you can elect another spokesman instead.'

Stacey had stopped crying. The history teacher gave her a handkerchief. Stacey mopped her cheeks with it. She didn't dare use a teacher's handkerchief to blow her nose.

'It'll take too long, getting all the rest of the class to see Tommy's no good at the job,' said Stacey. 'They don't even realize how horrible the English teacher's being!'

'Fighting is usually a boring and difficult business,' said the history teacher.

'But most of the class don't mind a bit about anyone else, they're only thinking of themselves!' mumbled Stacey through her swollen, stuffed-up nose.

'Blow your nose and don't sound so superior,' said the history teacher. 'Anyone can understand these things if you explain them enough!' Then he pointed to the headmaster's door. 'Or of course you could go and see the Head and complain of Mr Haberl. That's your alternative.'

'Is it the only alternative?' asked Stacey, venturing to blow her nose on a teacher's handkerchief after all.

'You could go home, go to bed and be ill,' said the history teacher, 'but I don't suppose that would appeal to your fighting instincts.'

Stacey made up her mind to go back to the classroom, but it was not easy. As she approached the classroom door, she thought: a guardian ghost's not as much use as a guardian angel! A guardian angel would be right beside me now, waving a lily in an encouraging way. But Rosa won't come out. She's dozing in the attic at home. (This was not true. Rosa was sitting in the kitchen with Mum, discussing life and death and a number of other things beyond ordinary human understanding.)

Stacey stopped outside the door. She could hear the English teacher's voice. 'Now, open your books.' She heard a rustling, and then his voice again. 'Page 102.' If the history teacher hadn't been waiting by the stairs, giving her an encouraging nod, she would have waited some time before she went in. As it was, however, she took a deep breath, opened the door, went in, said, 'Please, I didn't feel well,' and she went to her desk.

'I see!' said the English teacher, grinning. 'Too much agitation upsets sensitive young ladies!'

Stacey sat down, opened her English book at page 102, and pretended to be busy following the text the English teacher read out slowly, sentence by sentence. As she did so, she glanced around the class. Michael winked at her, Hans gawped in amazement, and Gerald seemed pleased about something. 'He gave Gerald a D after all!' Tina whispered.

The English lesson passed slowly, very slowly. Just before the bell rang, Stacey was asked to read a short paragraph aloud, and the English teacher praised her good accent, but Stacey was not pleased. She thought: he doesn't take my protest seriously! He doesn't care a bit what I say! He isn't even angry with me!

In break, before the last lesson, Stacey had a go at talking to Tommy, as advised by the history teacher. But he stuck to his guns, saying first that he didn't know his way around the Education Act, and then that Stacey was the only one who'd wanted him to protest. He mentioned Gerald's D by way of defending himself, since as he said, Gerald wouldn't have done any better than D in any case. 'And you saw what came of going on at him,' he added. 'Nothing. Absolutely nothing!'

Tommy and Stacey were surrounded by quite a crowd of children. Some of them nodded, agreeing with Tommy, but others nodded when Stacey said, 'That's no kind of argument! Teachers have to keep the law, that's the point!'

'Exactly!' said Michael. 'That's what I think too!'

'Gerald wouldn't get a better accent in just a few days, would he?' said Tommy.

'All very well for you to talk!' said Tina. 'You and your three hours' extra coaching a week!'

'It never hurts to be prepared,' said Gabrielle.

'That's right, go ahead, show off!' said Gerald. 'Swot!'

'I'm not a swot!' said Gabrielle. 'I do less work than you do!'

She punched Gerald in the stomach, and Gerald hit her. She pulled Gerald's hair, and Gerald kicked her shin. Hans tried parting them, Tina tried to help Hans, but somehow Hans and Tina found themselves punching and kicking and pinching too, and all of a sudden Tommy and Michael and Stacey were in the middle of the fight as well, and when the biology teacher came into the classroom she saw about a dozen scuffling children in a tangled heap, with another dozen or so standing around in a circle.

It was not easy to upset the biology teacher, and a few scuffling children did not seem likely to do the trick. She sat down at the teacher's desk and waited.

The onlookers, hesitantly, went to their desks. Tina noticed that the biology teacher was already in the classroom, and let go of Tommy's hair. To her dismay, Stacey saw it was Michael's arm she had been about to bite. This upset her so much that she withdrew, and then it was only a few seconds before the heap had untangled itself.

'Fight over?' asked the biology teacher, took the absence of any answer as an affirmative, and drew the skeleton of the domestic cat on the board.

Back in her desk, and breathing hard, Stacey took out her biology book, copied down the skeleton off the board and thought sadly: I don't suppose fighting is the way to get a real community spirit in the class. I must have gone wrong somewhere.

14

Stacey had a great deal to do that afternoon. She was planning to have a long talk with Dad about the Education Act, she was planning to talk to Mum about Rosa Riedel, and she was planning to talk to Rosa about her failure to get the whole class behind her. She was also planning to take the bedside rug, cushion and eiderdown up to Rosa at last, officially this time. She was going to draw Rosa a big picture in felt pen as well. It was to show a tram, and Rosa crossing the road, and Mr Fischer and the Nazi storm-troopers and the people who didn't go to Mr Fischer's aid. She intended to ask Mrs Berger just what Nazi stormtroopers and Viennese trams had looked like at that time, so as to get this picture quite right.

But it all turned out quite differently! When Stacey got home, she found that Uncle Egon and Aunt Erica from Linz had come visiting. (They had come to Vienna for a funeral, and were 'combining duty with pleasure', as Uncle Egon put it.)

So Stacey couldn't talk to either Mum or Dad. She just asked Dad quietly, 'Is Rosa up in the attic?'

'No, here!' Dad whispered back. He grinned. 'Aunt Erica sat down on her.'

'What happened?'

'Rosa squealed.'

'Then what?' Stacey drew Dad into the boxroom, closing the bedroom door so that she could raise her voice a bit more.

'Aunt Erica thought it was our sofa squeaking.'

'Was that all?'

'Far from it! Your uncle said something, something

political and damn stupid, and Rosa muttered, "Idiot!"'

'Then what?'

'Egon thought I'd said it. He's feeling rather insulted.'

'And where's Rosa now?'

'First she went into the kitchen and started cleaning the window. I asked her not to—I hope I haven't hurt her feelings. But if Egon or Erica had happened to go into the kitchen and seen the cloth rubbing away at the window all by itself, they could well have had a heart attack!'

Stacey went into the kitchen. 'Rosa?' she whispered. 'Are you there, Rosa?' Nothing stirred. Stacey looked at the window. One side of it was rather dirty. The other was shining bright and clean. In looking at the window, Stacey also looked through it and saw Tina at her own window on the other side of the yard. Tina waved. Stacey quickly ducked and took cover beneath the window-sill.

She didn't mind being friends with Tina again, but just at the moment it was an inconvenient friendship, since she didn't want to go down to the yard. However, if she told Tina that in sign language, Tina would be sure to feel cross again.

So Stacey crawled out of the kitchen on hands and knees. Not until she reached the hall did she stand up and go into the living room, where she found Mum, Dad, Uncle Egon and Aunt Erica eating cake and drinking wine. There was rather a deep dent beside Mum in the brown velvet of the sofa.

Uncle Egon was talking, saying that people today didn't know when they were well off, they had everything they could ask for and it made them discontented, it meant that young people and children in particular were ill-behaved and ungrateful and cheeky and impertinent.

Stacey kept her eye on the velvet sofa. Rosa Riedel was feeling restless. You could tell, from the look of that dent.

'Another war, that's what we need,' said Uncle Egon. 'That'd teach the young to know their place. Or conscription into labour service, at least!' And then he yelled, 'Ow! Ouch!' Grabbing his nose with both hands, he held on to it tight. His wife looked at him in alarm, Mum and Dad grinned surreptitiously at each other.

'Whatever is the matter, Egon?' asked Aunt Erica.

Uncle Egon took his hands away from his nose. 'A sudden pain!' he groaned. 'Terrible!'

'A pain in your nose?' Aunt Erica was surprised, for after all, the nose is one of those parts of the body that seldom hurt badly.

'As if somebody'd put it in a vice,' muttered Uncle Egon, rubbing his nose, and then he announced that the pain was getting better.

'It's your nerves,' said Aunt Erica. 'You always get so worked up when you're talking about the problems of the day.'

Uncle Egon protested. 'I don't get nerves!' he said. 'Nerves are only for creeps and weaklings!' Then he went on getting worked up about the youth of today and the rising rate of crime. You might have thought every child was a criminal nowadays. Dad defended children and young people.

'Idealists like you can't see what's staring them in the face,' said Uncle Egon. 'You should know the statistics if anyone does! Crime figures among the young show a horrendous rise!' Aunt Erica nodded.

'But those figures aren't for murder and armed robbery. They're only cases of petty theft,' said Dad.

'Only! Only!' cried Uncle Egon, his nose bright red. 'Only! That's how it all starts, my dear fellow. Chewing-gum from the supermarket yesterday, the savings bank today, murdering a cabby tomorrow!'

'Don't be ridiculous!' said Dad, who was beginning to lose his temper. 'Stealing chewing-gum is a stupid thing to do, gets children nowhere, and causes a great deal of trouble when they're caught. I know all about that! But then, in our younger days the stuff wasn't all laid out so temptingly in front of our noses! We were no better, we just didn't have the opportunity.'

Mum added, 'And you stole apples from the garden next door yourself, Egon dear! Even though our own apples were much nicer.'

'Taking apples is different, Annemarie!' said Uncle Egon.

'How's it different?' asked Mum.

'We were innocent children—we didn't see any harm in it!' Uncle Egon was looking quite emotional.

'Children nowadays see no harm in taking chewing-gum,' said Mum.

'Oh, don't they?' cried Uncle Egon. 'They're spoiled rotten, that's their trouble. I can tell just from looking at the children next door!'

'Egon, you're an idiot!' said Mum. Uncle Egon fell silent, his feelings hurt, and a deep soft voice said, in the sudden silence, 'My own opinion entirely!'

Mum and Dad bent their heads. Stacey put two fingers in her mouth and bit the nails. Uncle Egon, bewildered, looked round. Who shared his sister's opinion? Albert hadn't uttered a word: he was sure of that. And his dear Erica surely did not think him an idiot! Stacey? He was quite ready to believe it of the child! But her voice was higher. Nobody in this room had a deep, soft voice like that.

In his bewilderment, Uncle Egon picked up the wine bottle to pour himself some more. He filled the glass to the brim. He raised it to drink. The glass shook vigorously in his hand. With difficulty, he got it to his lips, but it was shaking so much that he couldn't drink.

'Egon, you shouldn't get so worked up it makes you tremble!' said Aunt Erica. 'It's really not worth it! You know your sister and her husband don't think as you do!'

'I'm not trembling! It's the glass trembling.'

'Oh, come, Egon!' Aunt Erica smiled indulgently.

Uncle Egon put the glass down without drinking from it. Stretching out his arm, he told her, 'Look at that! It's not, it is *not* trembling!'

At first the hand really was steady, but then it began shaking as if Uncle Egon had a bad attack of palsy. Horrified, he withdrew his hand and hid it between the seat and the back of his chair. Mum felt sorry for Uncle Egon. She did think he was an idiot, but you can still be fond of an idiot if he happens to be your only brother.

'I'll get some more cake,' said Mum, getting up, and she left the room. Out in the hall, she signed to Stacey to join her. 'Stacey, dear, I beg you—get Rosa up to the attic for the next hour or so!'

Stacey didn't want to. She said it was not very polite to Rosa. In fact, it was plain insulting, or anyway tactless! Sighing, Mum went into the kitchen to get more cake, and through the bright, clean half of the window she saw Tina standing at her own window, waving.

'I know what, Stacey,' said Mum. 'I've had an idea! Take Rosa down to the yard! Tina's yard, I mean. After all, it was once Rosa's yard. She told me she made that arbour herself, and she planted the creeper that grows over it. I'm sure she'd like to see the garden!'

Stacey nodded. This idea was neither tactless not rude and insulting. Stacey waved to Tina. Tina pointed an interrogative thumb downwards. Stacey nodded and turned her own thumb down.

Mum started singing. 'Rosa, Rosa, give me your answer, do . . . .'

'What's all that about?' asked Stacey.

'Signal between me and your mum,' said Rosa Riedel, beside her. 'We worked out if one of us sings "Rosa, Rosa, give me your answer, do!" that means, "Come here quick!" Good idea, right? So here I am. What's up?'

'I thought,' said Mum, slicing the cake, 'you might like to go down to your old garden with Stacey.'

'We could sit in the arbour,' said Stacey. 'And I'll get Granny Wokurka to come there too if you like. She likes talking to me. You'd enjoy listening to her, I'm sure you would.'

'Well, I've often fancied going down to my arbour, but I'm a bit scared, see?' said Rosa quietly. 'I'd be bound to have memories of when I was alive in that arbour. It might not be good for me.'

'Why not?' asked Stacey.

'I could turn all sentimental,' said Rosa. 'I mean, a sentimental ghost—that's downright silly!'

Uncle Egon's voice was raised in the living room. 'Where are you, Annemarie? There's no call for you to go disappearing into the kitchen when I only come visiting once a year!'

'Yes, well, let's go down to the garden!' said Rosa. 'I'd sooner risk feeling sentimental than listen to that fool any more!'

When Stacey and Rosa got down to the yard, Tina was already in the arbour. She waved a new Asterix book.

Granny Wokurka was standing near the carpet-beating frame, hanging washing on the line. 'Talk to her, would you?' Rosa whispered to Stacey. 'I'd like to hear her voice again!'

'Come on!' said Tina impatiently, but Stacey went over

to Granny Wokurka, and asked how she was, and what she'd been cooking today, and if she'd been to water the flowers in the cemetery, and when she could think of no more questions, she said, 'Mrs Wokurka, do come and sit in the arbour and tell us a story about the old days!' At first Granny Wokurka didn't want to, because she was really planning to watch a film on afternoon television, but when Stacey begged her again, she gave in. She went into the arbour with Stacey.

'So which story would you like today?' Granny Wokurka had about two dozen stories of 'the old days', and Stacey and Tina had heard all of them several times before.

Tina was not particularly keen on these stories, but she was proud that Stacey liked her granny. 'Tell the one about Mrs Sedlak shutting the landlady in the cellar!' suggested Tina, knowing that this was a favourite of Stacey's. Granny Wokurka nodded, and began:

'Well, there was a terrible feud between those two at the time, you see. It had gone on for months, and everyday when they met at the tap— because in those days, you see, even the landlady didn't have running water in her apartment—Well, whenever they met at the tap it flared up again! And it had all started over some silly little thing. I've an idea it was the key to the front door. Or was it the key to the attic?' Granny Wokurka always stopped to think at this point in her story, and yet she could never remember whether the feud had begun over the front door key or the key to the attic.

'It was over wash-days! Mrs Sedlak was supposed to change with the landlady,' a soft voice whispered in Granny Wokurka's ear, and suddenly she beamed all over her wrinkled old face and cried, 'Why, I remember now! It was over their wash-days they quarrelled! Mrs Sedlak was supposed to change wash-days with the landlady, and she didn't want to!' Granny Wokurka looked triumphant. 'There, not so senile after all, am I?'

Granny Wokurka went on with the story. Stacey was laughing all the time, because it really was a funny story, and Granny Wokurka told it well. No one noticed a deep, quiet chuckle mingling, several times, with Stacey's clear laughter.

15

After this Stacey was down in the yard with Tina whenever the weather was reasonably fine. For Rosa's sake, not Tina's. Rosa loved the arbour, and now said sentimentality was not such a bad thing after all. She was so keen on the arbour and the garden that she was quite downcast when it rained one afternoon. But mostly she made out that it was just for Tina and Stacey she wanted to go down to the arbour, because they talked about school there, and the trouble they had with the teachers and the other children, and Rosa said she needed to hear Tina on the subject too if she was to form a real picture of the situation. 'If I only get to hear what you think, Stacey, I only know the half of it, don't I?'

'No!' Stacey protested. 'Tina's fat and slow. She never gets really excited about anything!'

'And you're thin and go flying off the handle, dear, and you get excited about a sight too much!'

Dad did, in fact, go up to the school the Monday after Stacey's argument with the German teacher. His plan of soothing the German teacher's feelings and getting Stacey back into favour with her failed, because in the course of their conversation Dad repeated all the vulgar words the lady found so offensive, actually saying them out loud. She was shocked. She had never thought a man who worked at the Ministry of Education could do such a thing! Dad didn't even notice the shock waves he was setting off, and he could not understand why she suddenly seemed so cool and would say nothing but, 'Just as you think, Dr Sommer,' and, 'Of course, that is up to you, Dr Sommer,' and, 'I'm afraid I don't agree at all, Dr Sommer'.

Out in the corridor, before Dad left the school, he also ran into the English teacher, who clapped him heartily on the shoulder, saying, 'Why, if it isn't our old colleague!' (For Dad had been a teacher himself before he began working at the Ministry.) Dad flinched. He did not like being clapped on the shoulder. It never occurred to the English teacher that anyone might not care for it. 'Bright daughter you've got, old chap,' he said. 'Manning the barricades the other day, over the timing of tests and so on—ah, that's an educationist's clever child for you, they know everything!' And he winked at Dad. Dad looked back without batting an eyelid, which annoyed Mr Haberl the English teacher. 'The fact is, old chap,' he added, clapping Dad on the shoulder again, but less vigorously this time, 'I'd be up to date with those tests if I hadn't been laid low for a week—liver trouble, must have been something I ate, and how am I supposed to get all my testing done after that?' He sounded almost apologetic, but Dad could not think of anything to say. Dad just mumbled, 'Yes, difficult, difficult.' Mr Haberl clapped him on the other shoulder, the one he had hitherto spared, nodded and hurried off to the staffroom.

Dad left the school building, looked up at the sun and felt glad not to be a schoolboy or a teacher any more. He felt slightly ashamed too. He thought he should have said something firmer to Mr Haberl about giving proper notice of tests, and the rights of schoolchildren.

Dad decided that at least he would tell Stacey about the English teacher's liver trouble that afternoon. That would be easier, and might lead to a better understanding between the children and their teachers.

However, Stacey was not much interested in the English teacher's liver trouble. She had other troubles of her own at school. Since that difference of opinion arose in her class, it had been split into two bitterly opposed camps. You were either on Stacey's side or Tommy's side. Those on Stacey's side included Tina, Michael, Gerald, Herbert, Hans and several others. Tommy had more on his side than Stacey, but they were mostly people Stacey had never specially liked, so she was happy enough. She was less happy when Rosa Riedel asked, 'And what d'you do besides quarrelling?' She also said, when Stacey told her about school, 'I don't like it, ducky! If you want to get things done, you should stick together!'

'Well, Tommy and his side won't, not with us,' Stacey explained. 'They're just stupid! And mean, and idiotic, and—' Stacey ran out of nasty adjectives to describe Tommy's side properly.

'Don't be silly!' said Rosa.

'You don't know them! You've got no idea,' said Stacey.

Rosa stuck to her guns. 'Come on, Stacey love,' she said, 'you don't really believe more than half your class is stupid and mean and idiotic, and nobody's clever and nice but you and a couple of others! I hear the way you and Tina carry on—Tommy's a pig! Gabrielle squints! Herbert's a show-off with his rich dad! Johanna ought to see a psychiatrist! Inge's got knock-knees! That's how you two go on! And what's that got to do with the timing of your tests?'

'Nothing,' Stacey had to admit. 'But we can't help saying things like that, Rosa!' she added, by way of explanation. 'It's only natural!'

To which Rosa replied, 'You have to help it, though, ducky, or you'll lose sight of what you were really after!'

Stacey and Rosa went down to Tina's garden after one such conversation. Stacey wriggled through the gap in the fence and Rosa, grunting and groaning, made her way through too. Tina was just coming out of the building. 'Hans phoned just now, Stacey!' she called. 'He had a spitting duel with Tommy in the park!'

'What did I tell you?' whispered Rosa. 'How does this Hans spitting at Tommy help? Is that going to make you all stick together, eh?'

Stacey said nothing. For one thing, because she could not think of a good answer, and for another because she had to be on her guard with Tina, who had already said, once or twice, 'You want to watch out, Stacey! You're always talking to yourself. I thought it was only my granny talked to herself, being so old!'

There was an old country-style wooden chest standing on the gravel path in the middle of the garden, between the flower bed with the gnome pushing a wheelbarrow and the rose bed. This chest had a beautiful pattern of roses painted on it, and a date, 1714. There was a large, ornate key in the wrought iron lock. The lid of the chest was open.

'Hello, what's that?' asked Stacey, touching the chest with the toe of one shoe.

'Hey, mind that chest, Stacey!' said Tina. 'It's supposed to be ever so valuable, worth a fortune!'

And Tina told Stacey that the chest once belonged to a farmer in the Innviertel district of Upper Austria, and Mr Dobrovolny up on the third floor had bought it a few years ago. The chest stood in his hall, and Mrs Dobrovolny always described it as 'our prize possession'. But now the Dobrovolnys were short of money, because their son had embezzled some cash and Mr Dobrovolny paid it back, so they had to sell their antique chest. And a man, some very rich man, had already been to see the chest and paid a deposit. Only he didn't like the smell of the chest. It smelled of patchouli, and this rich man hated the smell of patchouli.

Stacey bent down and sniffed. The chest smelled like mothballs, like whole boxes full of mothballs, like a mothball factory!

'So they've put it out in the garden to air,' said Tina. And Rosa whispered happily into Stacey's ear, 'Oh my, patchouli! My favourite perfume! Haven't smelled patchouli in years! Oh, lovely, I'll just lie down in this chest a minute, ducky!' she whispered, before Stacey disappeared into the arbour with Tina. 'I want to soak up that patchouli perfume. Just rouse me when you go home, supposing I fall asleep!'

'Okay,' said Stacey.

'What's okay?' asked Tina.

Stacey, who had become quite good at lying, said she thought the scent of patchouli was okay: she couldn't see what the buyer of the chest had against it.

Stacey and Tina had only been in the arbour a few minutes, and had hardly got into their stride with sniping at Tommy and his friends, when Tina's mother called down from her kitchen window, 'There's yeast puffs just out of the oven, children! All crisp and hot—Granny made them!'

Stacey loved yeast puffs. Her own mother's never turned out well. Mum's yeast puffs were either hard as rocks, or they had a bit of unbaked dough in the middle, or they were too sweet or too greasy.

'Filled with plum jam?' Stacey called back up.

'With vanilla sauce, no filling!' Tina's mother called down.

There was no holding Stacey now. Yeast puffs with vanilla sauce were her idea of heaven! Stacey shot out of the arbour, across the garden, in at the yard door and up the stairs, with Tina panting along behind her. Tina felt the same as Stacey about yeast puffs with vanilla sauce.

Stacey and Tina feasted on yeast puffs and vanilla sauce until the baking tray and the jug of sauce were empty, and then Tina said, 'Aaah!' and Stacey said, 'Oooh!' They stretched their legs out in front of them and folded their hands over their distended stomachs.

'Like to go down again now?' asked Tina.

'I can hardly move,' said Stacey. 'I'm full to bursting!'

'Oh, come on!' said Tina. She looked down at the garden and said, 'Oh, the chest's gone!'

'Yes, they drove off with it a moment ago,' said Tina's mother.

Stacey leaped to her feet and rushed to the door. She did not explain why she was in a hurry, nor did she say goodbye, or 'Thanks for the yeast puffs'. She galloped down the stairs, her full stomach protesting at every step. Reaching the front door, she saw a sky-blue delivery truck driving round the corner.

Panting, Tina came up behind Stacey. 'Wild beasts after you or what?' she inquired. 'Why did you dash off like that?'

Stacey felt so miserable that she forgot to be careful. 'I think they've taken Rosa Riedel away too!' she sobbed.

'Who's Rosa Riedel, and who's taken her away?' asked Tina.

Stacey wiped a few tears from her cheeks, looked at Tina for quite a while, and then said, 'Tina, I have to go home now. It's very important. Please don't be cross this time. Please don't take it as an insult. If you want to be my real friend, then you have to understand.'

'Understand what?' asked Tina. 'If you won't tell me anything I can't understand it, can I?' And Stacey saw a cross and injured expression on Tina's face again. She couldn't help thinking of Rosa Riedel, who was always saying, 'You have to try and explain things to other people, you know! You have to get along with them and consider their feelings!'

Stacey went close to Tina. 'Tina,' she said quietly, 'Tina,

I'm sorry, it's hard to explain. You wouldn't understand, so I can't tell you.'

The expression on Tina's face was getting steadily crosser and more injured. She shook her head and said, 'You just don't like me. I've known you didn't for ages! You only play with me when you've nothing better to do!' She shook her head again, and her guardian angel pendant slipped out of the rolls of fat around her neck. Stacey looked at the pendant, and the fat-cheeked angel's face with the wings on its neck. 'Well, all right, Tina,' she said. 'You've got a guardian angel, and I've got a guardian ghost. Her name's Rosa Riedel, And I'm afraid she's inside the Dobrovolnys' chest.' Tina stared. Stacey took a step backwards. 'And if you say a word about it to a living soul, I'll never, never like you again, understand?'

Tina raised her right hand, stuck her fat forefinger and her fat middle finger up in the air, and said solemnly, 'I swear by the eyesight of my unborn children that I won't say a word to anyone.'

Mum, Dad and Stacey searched for Rosa Riedel all evening. It was just possible that Rosa had woken up in time to nip out of the chest. Mum, Dad and Stacey went all over the building, whispering, 'Rosa! Rosa, where are you?' They searched the attic, they even searched the cellar, and hoping that Rosa might have been shut into an apartment they rang all the doorbells and engaged people in curious conversations, to give Rosa a chance to escape.

Mum rang old Franz's doorbell, and asked if he could by any chance lend her a size 8 screwdriver.

Dad rang at refined Miss Dostal's door and asked if the postman had left a registered letter with her, and when she said, 'Aow naow!' and was about to shut the door, Dad got his foot in it quickly and asked if Miss Dostal was all right, was there anything she wanted, could he do anything for her today? Afterwards, Miss Dostal felt quite touched.

Stacey asked Mrs Berger if her telephone was out of order too. Theirs had been, she said, for the last hour. With the apartment door still open, she got Mrs Berger to go over to her phone and try it.

Then there were the Specht family and the Horak family, who also lived in the building. Dad knocked on their doors and asked if by any chance his old Uncle Adalbert had called that afternoon: Uncle Adalbert, he said, was missing from his old people's home.

No sign of Rosa Riedel!

Sadly, Mum, Dad and Stacey went back to their own apartment. 'I knew it!' Stacey sobbed. 'She's in that chest! She went to sleep and then the furniture removal men closed the lid!'

There were tears in Mum's eyes as she said, 'Oh, poor thing, and she's so scared of being shut up in small spaces!'

'Goodness knows when that rich man will open the chest!' wept Stacey.

'Perhaps he'll put it down in his cellar and not take it out for months,' said Mum.

'Well,' said Dad, emotional but determined, 'I'm going to get Rosa Riedel back. I swear I am!'

16

'This has got to be handled very cleverly, very, very cleverly,' murmured Dad. 'The first thing is to ring Mr Dobrovolny and ask him who bought his chest.'

He fetched the phone book.

'He'll say that's none of your business,' said Mum. 'He's not the friendly sort. I know him. He's been bitter ever since that business of his son.'

'Mrs Dobrovolny's nice, though,' said Stacey. 'She always stands up for us when the man on the first floor says we're too noisy out in the yard.'

Dad found the Dobrovolnys' number. He sat down by the phone and lit a cigarette. Whenever he was about to do something important but unpleasant, Dad had to smoke. Stacey brought him an ashtray and then held her forefinger under the number in the telephone book so that Dad would not dial it wrong. (Dad wouldn't have dialled it wrong anyway, but Stacey wanted to be helpful somehow or other.)

'What are you going to tell him?' asked Mum.

'I'll make out I'm from the Innviertel Local History Museum and say I'm interested in the chest. And when he says he's afraid he hasn't got it any longer, I'll tell him that's bad news, because we wanted to photograph the chest for our archives, and then he'll tell me the new owner's name.'

This was a good idea. The only trouble was that the Dobrovolnys were out. Dad tried every ten minutes or so, letting the phone ring ten times. 'They must come home some time!' he kept muttering imploringly. 'They must come home some time . . . .'

'Yes, of course they will,' said Mum, 'but you can't say

you're the Local History Museum at midnight. You're pretty late calling anyway, for a Local History Museum. I bet they're not so mad keen there they do overtime!'

Just as Dad was about to try the Dobrovolnys again, the phone rang. 'Dr Sommer speaking,' said Dad, picking up the receiver, and then he handed it to Stacey. 'Tina for you.' (Tina very rarely rang Stacey, and had never before rung so late at night.)

'Hello,' said Stacey. 'What is it?'

'Stacey . . . ' said Tina, hesitantly. 'Listen, Stacey . . . .'

'Yes?'

'What you told me this afternoon—did you mean it?'

'Yes,' said Stacey, feeling cross. If only she'd kept her mouth shut!

'You weren't having me on?' Stacey felt even crosser. What an idiot Tina was! Didn't understand anything, just making a nuisance of herself asking silly questions and blocking the line.

'If you really, truly did mean it, Stacey, well, I just wanted to say I know where the chest is.'

'You *do*?'

'Yes—but are you sure you're not pulling my leg? I mean—'

'Oh, come on, tell me!' Stacey shouted down the phone.

'Well, it's like this,' said Tina. 'I remembered I heard Mr Dobrovolny talking to Mr Schestak yesterday, out in the corridor.'

'Yes?' Stacey was fidgeting restlessly.

'They were talking about a "trip". Mr Schestak has a delivery truck, you see. So he drives things around delivering them. And Mr Schestak wanted to know if Mr Dobrovolny was paying for this trip.'

Stacey put two fingers in her mouth.

'And then Mr Dobrovolny said no, he was not paying for

the trip, Mr Filzmeier the engineer was paying on delivery.'

Stacey bit her fingernails. 'Hurry up, Stacey!' said Mum. 'We want to try Mr Dobrovolny again!' Stacey took her fingers out of her mouth and signed to Mum to keep quiet. 'Go on!' she said into the phone.

'Well, so just now, when you'd gone, I thought the only thing that he could be delivering was the chest. So I went round to Pepi Schestak and asked him if his dad had taken it away, and he had! Pepi was actually with him! He told me they drove quite a long way, and left the chest at a big detached house with a garden. There was an alsatian called Ludwig there, and some silver firs near the house, and a housekeeper called Berta. That was all Pepi knew, because he's so dim he doesn't notice street names.'

'Couldn't you ask his father?'

'He's gone to the pub with Mr Dobrovolny,' said Tina, 'but I don't need to ask, not now. I got out the phone book and the map of the city. There are eight Filzmeiers listed as engineers, but only three of them live in parts of Vienna where you'd find detached houses with gardens. So first I rang a Mr Filzmeier in Grinzing—'

'What on earth did you say?' asked Stacey in alarm.

'I asked if I could speak to Berta the housekeeper. But the lady who answered the phone said she was afraid she didn't have a housekeeper. So then I rang a Mr Filzmeier in Neuwaldegg, and I asked for Berta again, but the man who answered the phone said she'd gone home. I wanted to make quite sure it was the right place, so I said I was ringing about the dog. I made out I lived somewhere quite close, and I said a dog had got into my garden and I thought it looked like the Filzmeiers'. So then the man called, "Ludwig! Ludwig!" and whistled. Out of the window, probably. Then he thanked me very much but said he was glad to say Ludwig was in his garden, he could see him from the window. That must be the place, Stacey!'

'Oh, Tina, that was really nice of you!' Stacey was genuinely touched. She made up her mind never to be nasty to Tina again. She wouldn't even think cross things about her.

'That's all right, Stacey,' said Tina. You could tell from her voice how proud she was of her achievement. 'Right, listen carefully: this Mr Filzmeier's first name is Konstantin, and he lives at 43, Promenadenweg.'

Stacey reached for a pencil and a piece of paper and wrote it all down, including the telephone number: 69-29-44.

'I'll ring off now, then,' said Tina. 'Mum will be furious if she comes out of the bathroom and sees I'm still on the phone—our phone bill's always more than it ought to be.'

'Thanks, Tina,' said Stacey, but Tina had already rung off.

She showed Mum and Dad the note. 'That's where the chest is—it must be! Tina found out!'

'Did you tell her about Rosa?' asked Mum.

'Only that she exists and she's in the chest!'

'But she'll want to know more now,' said Dad.

'She certainly will!' said Mum, and then added, 'But if you ask me, Rosa will like Tina. She won't mind.'

'I mind, though!' cried Stacey. 'Rosa's *my* guardian ghost! And you two are sharing a bit of her already, and if Tina's in on it as well, that's too many! Anyway, Tina's got her own guardian angel!'

'Egocentric only child . . . ' muttered Dad. He picked up the note with Mr Filzmeier's address. 'And what do we do now?' he wondered.

'Ring up, of course,' said Stacey.

'Saying what?'

Mum and Dad and Stacey sat there for over an hour,

trying to think of reasons for asking Mr Filzmeier to open the chest immediately. But whenever one of them thought up a good story, the other two said, 'Ridiculous!'

By now it was nearly midnight. Dad was yawning, Mum was yawning, and Stacey, leaning against Mum's shoulder, was almost asleep.

'We won't think of anything now,' said Dad. 'This is pointless!'

'Let's leave it till tomorrow,' said Mum. 'I think best first thing in the morning.'

Stacey said nothing. She rubbed her burning, tired eyes, stumbled into her room and fell on the bed. 'Don't forget to get undressed, Stacey!' Mum called from the hall. 'Okay,' muttered Stacey. She undid her jeans and pulled them down. She got her right leg out of them, and then dropped back, exhausted, and fell asleep. She did not sleep for long, and she did not sleep well. If you are lying across your bed, legs hanging, jeans dangling from them, without any covers over you, you are unlikely to sleep soundly.

Stacey woke up, shivering. Her head ached and her legs had pins and needles. She switched on her bedside light. The alarm clock said eight minutes past one. Stacey took her jeans off her left leg, got into bed properly and covered herself up. However, she was unable to fall asleep again. She kept thinking of Rosa. Rosa now lying squashed into that chest, in panic terror. Stacey could positively feel the terror.

She remembered how frightened she used to be by herself on evenings when her parents were out. But Mum and Dad came home by midnight at the latest, Stacey said to herself. I never had to feel frightened for more than four or five hours! And Rosa had now been in a state of terror since afternoon. It would be unbearable to suffer panic terror for so long! You'd die of it! And if you couldn't die of it any more, it would send you crazy!

Rosa mustn't be sent crazy. Stacey sat up in bed. She put all four fingers in her mouth and bit their nails. And suddenly she had an idea. 'Here goes, Rosa,' she murmured.

Stacey stole out of her room and into the hall. Her parents' bedroom door was open. Stacey quietly closed it and went into the living room. She switched on the light and shut the living-room door too. She didn't want anyone hearing her. The note of Mr Filzmeier's number was still lying by the telephone. Stacey picked up the receiver and wrapped Mum's silk scarf, which was lying on the floor, round the receiver like a bandage. (She had once heard that a piece of fabric over the receiver changed your voice.) Then she dialled the number. The phone rang seventeen times before a sleepy voice answered, 'Filzmeier—hello? Hello, Filzmeier speaking!' Stacey was so excited she couldn't speak. 'Filzmeier—hello?' The voice was less sleepy now. Stacey tried to make her own voice sound grown-up and menacing.

'Mr Filzmeier, you bought a chest today—'

'I can't hear a word!' shouted Mr Filzmeier. 'Speak louder, would you? I can't hear you!'

The scarf round the receiver must be too thick. Stacey hastily unwrapped it and began again, 'Mr Filzmeier, go and open the chest at once!'

'Do what?'

'Open the chest or there will be a disaster!'

'Who is speaking?'

'That doesn't matter,' said Stacey, in as hollow and threatening a voice as she could manage. 'Open the chest or something will happen!'

There was silence for a moment at the other end of the line, and then Mr Filzmeier said, 'Look here, are you a child?'

'Children are asleep at this time of night,' Stacey informed Mr Filzmeier. 'Go and do it!' she urged him. 'Open the chest!'

There was another moment's silence, and then Mr Filzmeier said something extremely vulgar. Evan Rosa Riedel would not have put it in a composition! Then he hung up.

Stacey's heart was thudding. She was trembling slightly. But then she dialled again. This time the phone rang only ten times before Mr Filzmeier shouted, 'Is that you again? Let me sleep, will you?'

'You must open the chest first!'

Mr Filzmeier said the very vulgar thing again and hung up.

The third time, Stacey was no longer trembling and her heart had stopped thudding, and Mr Filzmeier reached the phone after it had rung four times. 'Have you opened the chest!' Stacey could say no more, because Mr Filzmeier repeated the same vulgar remark and rang off.

Stacey rang back to ask Mr Filzmeier if the chest was open seven more times. She heard the vulgar remark six times. He said it in a bellow twice, in a roar twice, and in a groan twice. The seventh time, Mr Filzmeier whispered, 'All right, all right, I'll go and open the damn chest! Even if it does make the whole house stink of patchouli. And then will you let me get some sleep?'

Stacey was so exhausted that she decided to take Mr Filzmeier's word for it. She staggered back to bed and fell asleep at once. Next morning, when she woke up, she remembered the whole thing, but she thought it was a dream. I'd never really dare do a thing like that, she thought, I'm far too cowardly! I'd only dare in a dream!

17

Dad came into Stacey's room in the morning, looking grim and determined. 'Anastasia,' he said (and Stacey could not remember Dad ever calling her by her full name before), 'Anastasia, do you think it would be right for us to do something illegal in Rosa Riedel's interests?'

'Do what?' asked Stacey.

'I've no idea exactly what it would be called, maybe false pretences or gaining entry by means of false representations, how should I know?' And then Dad said it would be no good just asking Mr Filzmeier to open the chest. 'He'd think I was crazy and call an ambulance to take me away!' So Dad decided to stick to his original idea of the Local History Museum. He was going to ask Mr Filzmeier if he could take a photograph for the museum's archives.

'What does Mum think?'

'She's gone to borrow Fred's super-camera.' (Fred was a friend of Dad's and mad about photography. He spent all his money on amazing pieces of photographic equipment.)

'I'll come with you,' said Stacey. 'Rosa will need me to comfort her. You wouldn't be good at that bit!'

Dad was against this. 'For one thing, you have to go to school—'

'And you have to go to the Ministry!' Stacey interrupted.

'And for another thing, photographers don't usually go about with children in tow.'

'I'll wear that stupid dirndl skirt Aunt Erica gave me,' said Stacey, 'and you can say I'm to be in the picture with the chest, for atmosphere.'

But Dad was still against it. 'Nobody would go putting a child in an archive photograph!' However, Stacey was already out of the room, and when she came back she was wearing her traditional Austrian calf-length dirndl skirt. 'And I'll put my hair up in a bun,' she called, disappearing again. When Mum came back with Fred's camera, Stacey was all ready. She looked like an Austrian peasant girl in costume out of a picture book. 'Darling, persuade her not to come!' Dad asked Mum.

'Why? She looks splendid!' And that decided it. 'But aren't you going to ring first, Bertie?' Mum asked. 'One would. I mean, photographers don't just turn up out of the blue!'

Dad was pacing nervously up and down the hall. 'Well, of course I know that! I'm not a fool!' he said, irritated. 'But suppose he says on the phone that I can't photograph his chest? Then I've no excuse for going to his house! Or suppose he says yes and rings the Innviertel Local History Museum back straight away? Some people are very suspicious!'

'He can't,' said Mum calmly. 'There's no such thing as an Innviertel Local History Museum.'

'Well, there you are!' said Dad, slinging the camera round his neck. 'Surprise tactics are the only way. Come on, Stacey!'

'Good luck,' said Mum.

'And once you've got Rosa back don't let her out of your sight!' Mum spoke as confidently as if there could be no doubt at all of Rosa's imminent return. (Mum could sometimes be a very good actress.)

'Can you actually work that camera?' asked Stacey, as they drove to Mr Filzmeier's.

'Well, I can click it,' said Dad. 'It doesn't matter what the film shows afterwards!'

'Dad, are you scared?'

'I don't really know,' said Dad. 'Ever since I had to accept that Rosa exists, I haven't had control of either my mind or my feelings!' And he added, quietly, 'Or I suppose I wouldn't be letting myself in for this ridiculous masquerade!'

Stacey recognized Mr Filzmeier's house at once. There were the silver firs, and Ludwig the dog putting his nose through the garden railings.

'This is sheer lunacy,' muttered Dad, getting out of the car.

It looked as if he were going to get back in the car and drive home again, so Stacey called, 'Come on, Dad! Every second in that chest must be torture for Rosa!'

'Okay.' Dad took Stacey's hand and walked to the garden gate with her. Then he spotted the large dog's muzzle poking through the railings. 'I say, Stacey, we can't go in,' he said hopefully. 'Look at that enormous dog! You don't like large dogs!'

'Rosa helped me get over being scared of dogs, Dad.' And Stacey opened the garden gate.

'She actually did that?' Stacey nodded. 'Right!' said Dad, as grim and determined as he had been that morning in Stacey's room. 'Here we go, then!' He was ready to risk anything for someone who had helped his daughter to get over her terror of dogs. He was ready to do more than gain entry into private premises by means of false representation, or whatever the misdemeanour he was about to commit might be called.

As Stacey and Dad made for the house, the dog came up, wagging his tail. He sniffed at their legs and then went off again. Dad was going to ring the bell, but Stacey whispered, 'The door's ajar!' Dad pushed it open. There was a huge hall inside, with enormous green plants standing about: rubber plants and palms and oleanders and gigantic cacti. And then, among the green plants, they saw a fat, red and blue checked behind. It belonged to a woman kneeling down to clean the floor between the plants. Stacey and Dad went up to the checked behind. 'Excuse me, please,' said Dad, politely addressing the behind. Stacey was glad that Dad'd voice sounded firm and perfectly normal. The behind backed out from among the plants: the woman stood up and turned around. This must be Berta, thought Stacey.

'I'm Dr Winter from the Innviertel Local History Museum,' said Dad. 'Is Mr Filzmeier at home? It's about his antique chest. We've been in touch with Mr Dobrovolny . . . .'

Dad spoke rapidly and fluently. He might easily have been stammering and stuttering. The woman was not listening. She was looking at Stacey, enchanted, exclaiming, 'Oh, what a dear little girl! Oh, how sweet! What a real little doll! Might be out of a toyshop, in that costume! Oh, isn't she a love!'

She could hardly get over it. Dad pushed Stacey into the background and stationed himself in front of her. The woman at last took some notice of him. 'What were you saying, then?' she asked. 'Come about the chest, did you? To photograph it, with the dear little girl, was that it? Oh, that'll make a lovely picture, that will! Such a sweet little thing!'

'Whereabouts is the chest?' asked Dad. He saw a chance of doing the deed without having to encounter Mr Filzmeier.

'Mr Filzmeier's still asleep,' said the woman. 'He had a terrible night, poor thing, never slept a wink, so he told me first thing this morning, and then he went back to bed.'

'Well, we mustn't disturb Mr Filzmeier,' said Dad. 'It won't take a minute. Whereabouts is the chest?'

The woman pointed to a door at the far end of the big hall full of plants. Stacey ran to the door. Suddenly she didn't care about anything except Rosa! Stacey flung the door open. There stood the chest, with its lid open. 'Rosa!' cried Stacey. 'Rosa, are you still there?'

All was quiet in the room containing the chest. It was not so quiet in the hall. A voice familiar to Stacey from last night's dream called, 'What's going on, Berta? I told you I wanted to get some more sleep! Who's there?'

'Oh, it's the man from the Local History Museum, and a lovely little girl!' Stacey heard Berta say. 'To photograph the chest, Mr Filzmeier!'

'Oh, for heaven's sake!' bellowed the voice out of Stacey's dream. There were now footsteps to be heard as well, and the voice out of Stacey's dream was no longer bellowing but asking plaintively, 'What the devil is all this about the damn chest? You want me to open its damn lid again, maybe? Well, come on, what is it, for God's sake?'

Evidently Dad was deprived of speech. Stacey left the room containing the open, empty chest and went back into the hall, but she hid behind the nearest green plant.

Dad had now recovered his powers of speech. 'Dr Winter of the Innviertel Local History Museum!' he introduced himself again, politely. 'Mr Dobrovolny referred me to you! It's about a photograph of your chest for our archives. We are anxious to ensure that our archives are complete.'

Mr Filzmeier was short and fat and bald, and he wore a pair of shiny pyjamas with pink and yellow stripes.

'As far as I'm concerned,' he said, 'you can take that chest away with you! I don't want it any more! Some idiot female rang me ten times last night, threatening disaster if I didn't open it! My son's off his head too! Crying until midnight because he said the chest was whimpering!'

Mr Filzmeier sat down heavily on a small stool, yawned, ran his hand over his bald head and turned to Berta.

'Would you believe it, there was I comforting the poor little fellow till twelve, telling him a chest can't moan and groan, maybe it can creak a bit but that's its lot, and no sooner do I get the lad calmed down and asleep, and I'm on my own way to bed, than the telephone rings, and there's that idiot female going on and on at me until I go and open the lid of the damn chest!'

'Ooh, how terrible!' said Berta, much moved.

'And then of course I get indigestion, with all the fuss and bother, and I can't find my tablets—'

'Bottom left in the bathroom cupboard,' said Berta.

Mr Filzmeier nodded. 'And when I finally find the tablets, and my indigestion's better, the lad wakes up again and comes into my room howling, saying the house is haunted. His door opened, he says, and somebody said, "Just you go on sleeping!" And then the door closed again.'

'Andy's not the fanciful sort!' Berta shook her head.

Mr Filzmeier propped his elbows on his knees and laid his head in his hands. 'So then I get Andy calmed down again, and let him sleep in my bed, while I sit there beside him feeling like death!'

'You poor thing!' said Berta.

Mr Filzmeier straightened up again, looked at Dad, yawned, and said, 'So what do *you* want with that chest? Sorry, I don't think I quite caught it the first time, I was too sleepy. What was it you said, Dr . . . Dr . . . ?'

'Winter,' said Dad helpfully, and he repeated his piece about the Local History Museum and its archives.

It is not wise to dismiss other people as simple just because they happen to be sleepy and depressed. Mr Filzmeier yawned again, and then he stood up, rubbed his eyes and inquired, 'You want to photograph the chest on behalf of a museum?'

'That's right,' said Dad.

'The chest I bought from Dobrovolny yesterday?' said Mr Filzmeier, making sure.

'That's right,' said Dad.

'And are you certain there's no mistake?' Mr Filzmeier narrowed his eyes, which no longer looked at all sleepy.

'Yes,' said Dad.

'And he's got this dear little girl with him,' said Berta. 'I wonder where she's got to? Such a sweet love!'

'Now listen, will you?' said Mr Filzmeier quietly, but firmly. 'Listen to me, Dr Winter or Summer or whatever your name may be! I have news for you! I bought Dobrovolny's chest for my son Andy because he liked it. That chest is no more than forty years old, a white elephant stinking of patchouli, made by some do-it-yourself enthusiast, and I can tell you I paid no fortune for it. Now I ask you, Dr Winter or Summer or whoever you are, I put it to you, what does the Local History Museum want with a chest like that?'

Dad went quite pale. He could think of nothing to say. Mr Filzmeier took a deep breath, and when he had enough breath to roar with, he roared, 'So now get out! Just get out, whoever you are and whatever you want, or I shall murder you, understand?'

'Stacey!' called Dad. 'Come here, Stacey!'

Stacey came out from behind her plant and ran to Dad, who grasped her hand and ran out of the door with her as fast as he could go, which was a good deal faster than Stacey could. She stumbled, and Dad hauled her up and dragged her on.

Ludwig the dog was deeply interested in all this. He barked and showed his teeth and chased the pair of them down the gravel path to the garden gate. Just before Ludwig reached Stacey's legs, they got to the gate, slipped through it and slammed it behind them.

They jumped into the car. Dad turned the ignition key. Mr Filzmeier was standing at his front door shaking his fists. Ludwig the dog was jumping up at the railings, barking dreadfully.

The engine started. Dad drove down the road. 'I hope to goodness,' Dad gasped, 'that man never sets eyes on me again!'

'Dad,' said Stacey. 'The chest was open! And Rosa wasn't there!'

'Dad,' said Stacey. 'I rang Mr Filzmeier in the middle of the night. I didn't actually mean to keep quiet about it, but this morning I thought it was just a dream!'

'Dad,' said Stacey. 'Poor Rosa must be wandering around somewhere on her old flat feet. And she won't be able to find her way home.'

'Anything's possible!' said Dad. 'I've run out of ideas. We'll just have to wait and hope for the best!'

Stacey decided to wait and hope for the best at home, not school. She did not feel as if she could possibly go to school now, in traditional Austrian peasant costume at that, and with her hair in a bun.

'Oh, all right,' said Dad. 'I suppose if everything's all upside down we needn't bother about your education either!'

He drove home and let Stacey out of the car. 'Give my love to Mum,' he told her, and then he drove off to the Ministry.

Mum must have been waiting at the front door. It was open even before Stacey had hold of the handle.

Mum looked at Stacey, looked down the stairs, saw that Dad was not there, and asked her, 'No luck?'

'No,' said Stacey. 'None at all!'

'Then you'd better go to bed, dear,' said Mum sympathetically.

Stacey went to bed. She did not begin to cry until she was in bed, all tucked up, with two pillows under her head and Mum's hand stroking her cheek.

18

Stacey cried for two hours, and slept for two hours, and was then woken by the shrill sound of the doorbell ringing. Perhaps Rosa's found her way home, she thought. But it wasn't Rosa: it was Tina to ask if Stacey was at home, sick.

'She isn't feeling too well,' Mum told Tina. 'See if you can cheer her up a bit!'

Tina went into Stacey's room and sat down in the rocking chair. 'Did you do anything?' she asked.

'Yes, we went to see Mr Filzmeier!' Stacey had tears in her eyes again. 'The chest was open and Rosa had gone.'

'Then she'll soon be here. I mean, ghosts just fly around, right?'

'Not Rosa,' said Stacey. 'She has to walk on her old flat feet, and people tread on them because they can't see her!'

Tina looked surprised. Stacey hesitated briefly, and then she said, 'All right, you really are a good friend. I know that now!' Tina's double chin quivered with pleasure, and Stacey told her all about Rosa, from the red pressure marks on Tina's own raised arm to the patchouli perfume in the chest, and ending with Mr Filzmeier's furious outburst.

When Stacey had finished Tina told her for goodness' sake to calm down. 'She can't die any more, and she'll find her way back some time!'

'But think how scared she must have been! And think of her poor flat feet!'

Tina knew nothing about being scared, but she had flat feet herself, so she knew that you can walk quite a long way, even if your feet are flat. But she didn't wish to appear heartless, and she certainly did not want to lose Stacey's sudden approval of her. So she said, 'Poor Rosa, poor,

poor Rosa!' in tones as heartfelt as possible.

After this Mum, Dad and Stacey tried to go back to leading a normal life. They did not mention Rosa any more. Stacey went to school, came home, did her homework, went to play in Tina's yard, watched TV, read, cleaned her teeth and went to bed.

And yet the life of the Sommer family was not really normal at all. If they were all together, and there was the slightest sound anywhere, they held their breath until they realized it was just Mrs Berger knocking in a nail, or Miss Dostal closing the door. And every evening, just after nine, Dad would steal down to the front door of the building, which Mr Horak had locked a few minutes earlier, and unlock it again. And Mum wedged the boxroom window open to keep it from shutting by accident. And every morning all three of them quietly went all over the apartment whispering, 'Rosa, Rosa!' Mum went up to the attic three times a day 'to look at the washing'. Dad never sat down on a chair without feeling the seat of it first. Stacey kept opening the doors of all the cupboards 'to give them a bit of an airing'.

When Rosa Riedel had been gone for over a week, Stacey's misery turned into a sad, listless melancholy. The difference of opinion in her class no longer interested her. She did not mind if the English teacher tested someone he shouldn't, and she had no more trouble with the German teacher now she was writing her own compositions. Nor did she enter into anything else that went on at school. A sad person is not much interested to know that the catches of all the classroom doors have been replaced, because the doors were in such a bad state they had started blowing open at the least little draught. It leaves such a person cold to hear everyone saying that during Form 8a's geography period, when the geography teacher was going on about

South Africa, somebody said, quite loud and clear, 'Narrow-minded racist!' Stacey just told Tina, 'They must be a brave lot in 8a!' And when Tina said, 'But they say it wasn't them, they didn't know who said it!' she replied, 'Whoever did would be a fool to say so!'

'No,' said Tina. 'They really didn't know! They were all worked up! It was a voice they'd never heard before.' But Stacey had already turned away and was deep in melancholy again.

There was one thing she did notice, however. Hans had stopped stammering when it was his turn to answer questions. And when it came to tests, he could remember everything he'd known in break. In so far as a melancholy child can be glad of anything, Stacey was glad of that. One day she even noticed Hans chuckling as he went up to the board. At break she asked him, 'How come you're not frightened any more?'

'I don't really know,' said Hans. 'But I keep thinking of such funny things these days it makes me laugh.'

And then, during maths one day, Stacey was startled out of her melancholy. The maths teacher was a nice man, not at all strict or unfair or moody. The children in Stacey's class liked him all right, but they often behaved badly in his lessons, especially when it had been English just before maths. They kept their mouths shut in Mr Haberl's lesson, being scared of him, and opened them twice as wide in maths to make up for it. They laughed and talked, and when the maths teacher said, 'Quiet, please!' they took no notice, knowing he never took their names down or handed out punishments or sent anyone to see the Head.

There had been English before this particular maths lesson. Mr Haberl had been shouting all through English. (His liver was bothering him again.)

Gerald and Gabrielle in particular were being a nuisance

in maths. At first they simply talked to each other, then they ate chocolate and threw little balls of silver foil about. The maths teacher tried in vain to control them. 'Gabrielle, Gerald, please stop that,' he asked. As long as he kept his eye on them they stopped throwing silver foil and giggling. But as soon as he turned round to the board, Gabrielle picked up her red eraser, took aim at the maths teacher's back, and let fly. It did not reach him. In mid-flight, it suddenly turned and whizzed back through the air to Gabrielle, hitting her forehead.

'See that?' whispered Tina.

Everyone in the class had seen it. Everyone was rather baffled and bewildered. But Stacey sat there very straight, tense as a cat outside a hole with a mouse inside it. Only Rosa could do that, she thought. Rosa must be here! And if Rosa's here, she'll come to me!

Stacey sat there like a cat outside a mousehole for some minutes, by which time the rest of the class had calmed down again, and then she felt something soft and warm beside her cheek. Stacey relaxed, and leaned back, and Rosa Riedel whispered in her ear, 'Well, how are you, ducky? Worried about me, were you?'

Stacey nodded.

'I'm fine, ducky! It wasn't so very bad in that chest. I had the scent of patchouli to soothe me!'

Stacey stood up. 'Please, I need to leave the room!' The maths teacher nodded. Stacey groped for Rosa's hand and pulled her out of the classroom.

'You might have waited till break, ducky!' said Rosa, once outside. 'You're missing fractions!'

'I couldn't care less!' said Stacey, taking Rosa into the cloakroom.

'I could, though,' murmured Rosa. 'Never was any good at fractions as a girl. I fancy catching up with them now!'

Stacey pushed Rosa into one of the lavatory cubicles and locked the door. Rosa sat on the lavatory bowl. Stacey sat down cross-legged on the floor. 'Come on, tell me what happened, Rosa!' she demanded. 'How come you're here? I can't make it out!'

So Rosa told her tale.

'Well, I woke up when Dobrovolny closed that chest. But I said to myself, nothing you can do about it now, I said, you'll just have to see how you cope with that phobia of yours, won't you? The patchouli was a big help. Why, I even dropped off to sleep again after a bit. So when I woke up I heard voices. A man's voice and a child's voice. Well, I thought, I'll just wait till the man's gone and then I'll talk to the boy. It's easier talking to children. That was a mistake, though! When I got the lad to notice me he yelled the house down. Oh, he was a terrible child, he was! I spoke to him ever so nicely, but he just yelled worse and worse. So back came his dad, and the boy wept, "The chest's moaning!" His dad—man by the name of Filzmeier, so I found out later—his dad tried to talk him out of it. "Come, come, Andy." Went on like that for hours, and then this Andy finally went to sleep and his dad left the room. I reckoned I'd just have to stay in that chest all night, but the phone kept on ringing, and all of a sudden in comes this Filzmeier and grabs hold of the chest and drags it out of the room. So there's me, bumping along the floor, and Filzmeier muttering, "Open the chest! I ask you! Well, anything to calm that idiot woman down! Not in Andy's room, though, oh no! I'm not having him fall sick on me on account of that reek of patchouli!" And then the lid opened and I was free.

'First I thought I'd go straight home, ducky, but I was scared I'd get lost, you see, in the middle of the night. I waited till it was light, and seeing as I was bored, I looked through young Andy's school books, and I found out he goes to the same school as you. So then it was easy! When Andy went to school, I just grabbed hold of one corner of his satchel and followed him! Down three streets, into a tram, off the tram again four stops later, change to another tram, two more stops, out again and up three streets and here I am!'

Rosa stopped.

'You mean you've been here over a week?' said Stacey.

'That's right,' said Rosa.

'Then why didn't you come and find me?'

'Ducky, I was looking for you that first day like you were a needle in a haystack, but you weren't around.'

'I was home, sick. Because of you.'

'And the second day I saw you, and kept trying to get to you, but it was too dangerous in lessons, and in break too. You children run about so, it scares me silly! Things were different when I was a girl! My school was a proper graveyard compared to this place here!'

'And you're not frightened now?'

'Not much!' said Rosa, proudly. 'I've got used to it, see? I keep very close to the wall where nobody can run me down or kick me.'

'But why didn't you come and find me later?'

'I've been in your class quite a bit, dear, but young Hans needed me, see? Oh, I've had my hands full with young Hans! And there's that nice maths teacher to be looked after, and I've had to pinch the English teacher a good few times when he was in a nasty mood.' Rosa was becoming increasingly excited. 'I tell you what, ducky, I'm not past it yet! I've been around more this past week than in the last thirty years put together! Why, I even went home with young Hans. I had a word with his mum, and gave his dad a good fright! He won't bother the lad any more, I can tell you!' Rosa sighed contentedly.

'And now what?' asked Stacey.

'Well, now I must get up to that lab,' said Rosa, 'because 7b are being so nasty to the new chemistry teacher, he's near tears after the lesson. And then I'm off to 3c to tickle the Latin teacher and make him laugh for once. And at twelve I'll be at a disciplinary meeting, about that little fair girl in 4b it is, and I'll have to keep her form teacher up to scratch. He's on the girl's side, see, but if I'm not there he won't dare speak up for her against the rest of the staff.'

'Then what?'

'Then I'll have my nap—I'm living down in the cellar with the boilers now—so as to be in good shape for gym this afternoon. I'm planning to get Tina up that rope and wipe the silly grin off Mr Haberl's face.'

'But you can't climb a rope yourself,' said Stacey.

'Ducky, I'll tell you something,' whispered Rosa. 'A secret, mind. I reckon I'm learning to float again! I already floated over the big table in the staffroom. What do you say to that, then?'

Stacey said nothing. She stood up and unlocked the lavatory door.

'See you in the gym this afternoon, right?' said Rosa. Stacey nodded and left the lavatory, followed by Rosa. 'Not cross with me, are you, ducky?' Stacey shook her head. Rosa was surrounding her, all soft and warm. 'Tell you what, if you need me just sing, "Rosa, Rosa, give me your answer, do." How's that?' Stacey nodded. And then the soft warmth of Rosa was gone. Stacey went back to the classroom and sat down at her desk.

'Aren't you feeling well?' asked Tina.

Stacey took a piece of paper out of her pocket. 'Rosa Riedel's guardian ghost of this school now!' she wrote.

Tina put the note on her side of the desk, grinned all over her fat face and wrote, 'That's great!' on the paper.

Stacey took it back, staring at the words, and they swam before her eyes, because her eyes were full of tears. Then she heard a very quiet voice saying, 'Egocentric only child . . . .' Stacey did not know if it was Rosa's voice, or the memory of Dad's voice when he was sitting by the phone trying to ring Mr Dobrovolny. But she answered the voice, just as quietly. 'No, I'm not!'

Then, underneath Tina's 'That's great!' she wrote, 'Yes, great for all of us!'